Rehearsing for Murder Can Be Fatal – A Senior Sleuthing Club Cozy Mystery – Book 9

by

Jinty James

Rehearsing for Murder Can Be Fatal – A Senior Sleuthing Club Cozy Mystery – Book 9

by

Jinty James

DEDICATION

To the real Teddy, my wonderful
Mother, Annie, and AJ.

CHAPTER 1

"I can't believe we're gonna have our first acting lesson!" Martha Mayfield's eyes sparkled with excitement and her gray curls sprang around her face. Dressed in a turquoise track suit, she looked like she was on her way to a senior activity, not waiting for a Hollywood actress to appear on her doorstep.

"Is she here yet?" Zoe asked. Her brunette pixie cut had a few strands sticking up, as if standing to attention.

"Not yet," Pru Armstrong reported. "I've just looked out the front – again."

"It will definitely be interesting to meet Tandy Tabor," their friend Claire said. Tall, blonde, and athletic, she wore black yoga pants and a fuzzy blue sweater. "I wish Molly could be here, but she's tucked up in bed right now." She spoke of her daughter who was currently in elementary school.

"Won't Tandy be surprised when she sees us all?" Martha rubbed her hands in glee. "Thank you all for coming – it means a lot."

"You're welcome." Lauren smiled. She, along with her cousin Zoe, ran the Norwegian Forest Cat Café in the small town.

"I'm looking forward to seeing her," Brooke, the local hairstylist, spoke. Her chestnut locks, cut in a long bob with feathered ends, had attractive reddish highlights. The hair color flattered her friendly green eyes. "There was an old show on TV last week, and she had the starring role! I couldn't believe it when I saw it."

"When was this?" Doris pushed a limp strand of hair off her brow. She wore comfortable looking jeans and a green sweater.

"Last Thursday," Brooke replied. "It was a sitcom about a single mom raising a family."

"We can ask her about it when she arrives." Martha grinned.

"Ruff!" Teddy, Martha's small, white Coton de Tulear, agreed, a big smile on his furry face.

Martha had written a TV series about a retired lady detective who solved police cases that the two young not so hot shot detectives at her old station couldn't. Martha had even gained an agent, Trish, but so far Trish hadn't been able to sell the series to anyone.

That hadn't deterred Martha, though. She'd come up with the idea of making the TV show herself, with the help of a library book her friend and roommate, Pru, had given her.

Trish had been intrigued with the idea, and had recommended they take acting lessons.

Not only that, but Martha had created roles in the episodes for her friends. Since Pru led a yoga class every Tuesday night in the church hall, it had seemed natural to include everyone from that class in the show.

That meant Martha had written six episodes, and Pru, Lauren, Zoe,

Claire, Brooke, and Doris had their own part in one of them.

"Ruff! Ruff!" Teddy darted toward the front door at the sound of an approaching vehicle.

"That must be her!" Martha barreled her rolling walker after him.

By the time Pru reached the front door, Martha was already opening it.

"It's her! It's her!" Martha made her way onto the porch and waved.

Car headlights punctured the black January night. A few stars twinkled in the velvet sky, and a street lamp down the road cast an orange glow on the cottages and houses that lined the street.

Some were original Victorian and some were faux, like Martha's duplex, although the other side had been vacant for a couple of months now.

A woman of medium height gracefully got out of the black sedan and strolled toward them. She wore tailored gray slacks, a cashmere sweater in the lightest of pink, and a tasteful gold necklace decorating her slim neck.

"I'm looking for Martha Mayfield." Her voice was smooth and cultured. "I'm Tandy Tabor."

"That's me!" Martha waved at her. "I'm Martha. And this here is Pru, and Teddy."

"Ruff! Ruff!" Teddy wagged his tail like a helicopter propellor, and parted his lips in a doggy smile.

"It's a pleasure to meet you." Tandy smiled, looking a lot younger than her reported sixty-plus years. Her face was wrinkle free and a little plump as if her skin had just been refreshed, but she looked very attractive. Her blonde hair was expertly cut and styled in a chic bob, the length perfect on her.

"Let me introduce everyone else," Martha said eagerly. "We've got Lauren, and Zoe – they run the café and you've gotta try their cupcakes and coffee. Then there's Brooke, who is the best hairstylist ever, so make sure you visit her salon while you're here. And this is Claire, who likes doing sporty things and is real good at them. And Doris, who works at

5

Gary's Burger Diner and is a real trouper. And of course, my pal Pru, who works at the library, but one day she's gonna be the head honcho of all the libraries in California. She's also my roomie. And this is Teddy, my dog, who loves playing games and is real good company."

"Ruff!"

"He's delightful." Tandy reached down, and then hesitated. "May I pet him?"

"Go for it," Martha told her, "but not on the head. On the shoulder."

"Wuff." Teddy accepted the soft caress and brushed against Tandy's pants.

"Oops, he's put a bit of fluff on you," Martha said apologetically.

"No problem." Tandy brushed the soft bit of white fur off her smart slacks.

"Let's go inside. We can't have you standing out in the cold night air." Martha ushered her inside the small duplex.

"We thought we could have the lessons in the living room," Pru said once they all gathered in the cheery room. There was a large yellow sofa and matching armchairs in the center, along with a coffee table.

"Mm," Tandy replied, glancing around.

"Trish did tell you there'd be a few of us, didn't she?" Martha asked a touch anxiously.

"Yes." Tandy nodded, her chic bob highlighting her expertly applied but subtle make-up. "That is not a problem. But the space might be. We'll be doing some warming up exercises, as well as role playing and going over your scripts. I'm not sure if this space will be big enough."

Martha's expression fell.

"I'm sure we can manage something," Tandy added hastily. "Don't worry."

"Would you like something to drink?" Pru asked. "Have you come straight from Los Angeles or did you stop at the motel first?"

"I went to the motel and freshened up," Tandy replied. "But a cup of coffee would be nice."

"Coming right up!" Martha barreled to the kitchen, Teddy following by her side.

"I can't believe you're here!" Zoe grinned. "We're so lucky Trish was able to get you!"

"You're Zoe?" Tandy looked at her.

"Yep!"

"Trish mentioned you," Tandy replied. "She said it was a shame you hadn't written any more scripts. She loved your princess movie, and so did I, by the way."

"Really?" Zoe looked like she was going to have a fan girl moment. "Wow! But you probably know they decided not to make any more of those movies, and I'm not a gritty western kind of person, and that seems to be the in thing at the moment. Now I'm making pottery mugs for the café and painting my own designs on them."

"They sell out quickly," Lauren put in.

"You must show me." Tandy smiled.

"We will! How about a cupcake and cappuccino on the house?" Zoe glanced at Lauren, who nodded.

"We'd love to have you visit. Annie, my cat, will lead you to your table and talk to you."

"Now that is something I'll have to experience."

"Here we are." Martha trundled through from the kitchen, the cup of coffee balanced on her black vinyl walker seat. Nice and hot, fresh from the pot!" She handed it to Tandy, then looked around at everyone else. "Oops. Does anyone else want one?"

"I'm good," Brooke said.

Pru noticed Doris hesitating.

"How about a hot chocolate? It's from a mix, but like Martha says, it's not bad," she offered.

Everyone suddenly said yes, and Pru found herself in the kitchen making hot chocolate for everyone while Martha entertained Tandy in the living room.

"Can I help?" Doris came into the kitchen.

9

"That would be great." She smiled at her friend. "I'll make them and you can take them out."

"It's exciting having Tandy here," Doris said, "but I don't know what to say to her."

"I understand." Pru felt that way herself. "But I'm sure Martha will say enough for both of us."

They laughed.

"I can't believe Martha has accomplished so much," Doris continued as Pru poured hot water into each mug and mixed up the cocoa concoction. "It makes me feel – I don't know – like I'm not doing anything with my life."

"Don't forget Martha is retired and doesn't have to earn a living anymore," Pru said. "She has plenty of leisure to work on her TV show, and I'm glad she's got an interest like that. I find I don't have much time for anything extra after working at the library and yoga."

"What about Jesse?" Doris sneaked a peek at her.

She blushed.

"I think it's the same for him, with his police work." She'd been dating the detective for a few months now, but sometimes it was hard to see him since they both had busy schedules.

"And your involvement in Martha's senior sleuthing club," Doris continued.

"That just happens," she replied.

"I hope it doesn't happen now," Doris replied. "I think it's great that you and Martha and Teddy discover the killers before the police do, but I'm really looking forward to these acting lessons. It will be something totally different!"

"I know." Pru smiled at her. "I feel that way too. And if Martha can actually make her first script into a real TV episode, that will be amazing."

"Won't it!" Doris picked up two steaming hot mugs. "I just can't wait!"

Once everyone had a cup of hot cocoa, they got settled and looked expectantly at Tandy, who sat on the yellow sofa. Pru found herself perching on one of the kitchen chairs brought into the living room, but she didn't mind. She was full of admiration for Martha and her determination to get things done. Six months ago, she would have found it hard to believe that one day she would take acting lessons from a Hollywood actress, and now here she was, along with her friends.

"What's it like being an actress?" Zoe asked.

"Fabulous!" Tandy smiled. "When everything is going well, it's the best job in the world. But there have been times when I've been out of work, and not sure when I'm going to get my next role. That can be dispiriting."

"I can imagine," Pru sympathized.

"Have you read my scripts?" Martha asked eagerly.

"The first episode," Tandy said. "I read it last night. I drove down here from Hollywood – I thought it would be fun to take a road trip. I love your retired lady character, Martha. If I wasn't booked to make this TV pilot, I would be asking if I could play that role."

"Really?" Martha looked flattered. "I would love you to play her but …" she paused.

Pru glanced at her and nodded encouragingly.

"I sort of thought I would like to play her myself," Martha finished in a rush.

After a moment, Tandy nodded. "I can just imagine you as her. You definitely have an imagination, Martha, and although I've just met you, I think you share some of the same traits as your lady detective."

"That's why Trish thought it would be a good idea to get some acting lessons," Martha added. "I wanna make this series myself, but how can I afford to pay real actors? Especially of your caliber. That's why I thought it would be fun if all of my friends could have a part in the series."

"Even if we crowdfund and raise some money, it might not be enough to pay all the real actresses and actors we'd require," Pru said.

"And you'll need the money for other expenses." Tandy nodded.

"Is it actress or actor these days?" Claire suddenly asked. "When I read an article in a magazine when I'm waiting in line at the supermarket, even actresses are called actors."

"I used to be called an actress when I started out, but everyone's called actor now," Tandy replied. "So everyone's equal." Tandy set her mug down on the coffee table in front of her. "Well, shall we get started?"

"Yeah!" Martha nodded so vigorously, her springy gray curls bounced around her head.

"Ruff!" Teddy agreed, sitting on the floor at Martha's feet. Martha sat next to Tandy on the sofa.

"What do we do?" Doris asked hesitantly.

"First, we stand up and stretch." Tandy demonstrated. Pru noticed that she had wonderful posture, her back straight and elegant.

"Then what?" Zoe asked eagerly.

"We shake our arms gently, then our legs." Tandy demonstrated. Somehow she still looked elegant, and not silly.

Everyone copied Tandy, then looked expectantly at her for the next instruction.

"Now we'll concentrate on our breathing."

"We do that all the time in Pru's yoga class." Martha chuckled.

"Excellent." Tandy smiled. "That will make things a lot easier."

"We're not going to do that trust exercise where you have to fall backwards and trust someone is going to catch you, are we?" Doris sounded worried.

"Not if you don't want to," Tandy reassured her.

"Oh, good." Doris let out a sigh of relief, echoed by some of the others.

"When do we get to start acting out my first episode?" Martha asked eagerly.

"I know I'm only here for a week, but I thought we could cover some of the basics first," Tandy explained. "Then we'll get to your script, Martha. Don't worry."

Now it was Martha's turn to look relieved.

By the time they'd done Tandy's warm up exercises, there was a buzz of laughter in the room.

"Now I understand what you meant about needing a bigger room," Martha said.

The armchairs had been pushed back and the only furniture still in its place was the sofa and the large screen TV.

"What about the church hall tomorrow night?" Pru suggested. Turning to Tandy, she explained, "We usually have yoga class there on Tuesdays so it won't be a problem."

"And the hall is much bigger than here." Lauren looked apologetically at Martha.

"I'm sure Father Mike won't mind," Martha put in. "Hey! What if we can use the church hall every night?"

"That's a great idea." Pru smiled. "I'll call Father Mike right now and see if it will be available."

"Wonderful." Tandy gave her an approving nod. "Thank you, Pru."

She dashed into her bedroom to grab her phone and dialed the

Episcopalian priest's number. Luckily, the hall was available for the rest of the week, and he waived her offer to pay the usual ten-dollar nightly fee.

"I think it's impressive that Martha is trying to do this," Father Mike told her. "I'm all for it."

Pru thanked him and ended the call. She hurried back to the living room, a big smile on her face.

"Woo hoo!" Martha didn't wait for her to explain. "There you are, Tandy."

"It's going to be awesome!" Zoe grinned.

"You mean it's not awesome already?" Lauren teased gently.

"It definitely is!" Zoe looked over admiringly at Tandy.

"Why, thank you." Tandy looked flattered at the praise.

"You must be used to people coming up to you in Hollywood and telling you how much they like watching you in your shows," Martha said.

"Not so much lately," Tandy said wistfully. "But when I was in that sitcom about the single mom, then yes, I used to get stopped at the supermarket sometimes. It's just a shame the show wasn't a big success."

"I saw it last week," Brooke offered. "You were great in it."

After a few minutes of reminiscing about that show, Tandy shook her head. "You paid me to give you acting classes, not talk about my past success."

"But it's so interesting," Zoe told her.

"It is," Doris nodded.

Tandy glanced at her watch. It had a pale pink strap and a pretty gold interface.

"I love your watch." Claire admired it.

"Thank you." Tandy smiled. "I couldn't resist buying it. Now, let's have another hour," Tandy said. She turned to Martha. "Is that okay with you? It's not too late?"

"Of course not," Martha replied stoutly, although Pru detected a hint of weariness in her tone. "That's what we're here for!"

"I know." Tandy sank down on the sofa. "Why don't we all sit down and do a reading of your first episode, Martha? How many of you are going to act in this episode?"

"Me." Martha brightened at the suggestion. "And Teddy. I wrote him a part specially, because maybe he'll be scooped up by Hollywood and become a big fancy star and we'll drive around in a red convertible and wave to everyone along Sunset Boulevard, and he'll get paid millions to be in a big movie, but he'll still prefer to act in my TV series. And Trish can be his agent, and I'll be his manager – co-manager – with Pru."

"Thanks." Pru smiled.

"That is certainly a vivid picture." Tandy nodded. "Okay. Who else is going to be in this first episode?"

"Doris." Martha pointed at her.

"Me?" Doris's mouth parted.

"Yeah, you're the waitress who shows my retired lady detective the way out of the restaurant when she's in a tight spot. It's totally you."

"Because I work at Gary's Burger Diner?"

"Because you're the type of person who will help someone out like that, even if she's a stranger. And yeah, because you know what it's like to work in a restaurant, so if I've written something wrong in the script, you can tell me and we can fix it together."

"Okay." Doris sat back in the armchair, looking pleased.

"You'll be awesome," Zoe reassured her.

"You will." Lauren nodded.

Pru grabbed the scripts Martha had printed out the week before and handed them around.

After flicking through her copy, Tandy assigned everyone parts. "Zoe, you can be one of the not so hot shots."

Everyone giggled.

"And Pru, you can be the other."

"Thanks – I think."

"It's a shame we don't have any men here to read the male parts," Tandy mused.

"Pru could call Jesse," Martha suggested mischievously. "He's her beau. And he's a police detective."

"Really?" Tandy looked impressed. "That is a great idea, Martha. Pru, can you—"

"I don't think so," she replied quietly.

"Why not?" Martha pouted.

"Because he's working tonight, and I don't know how he'd feel about it, anyway."

"You mean you haven't discussed this with him?" Zoe frowned. "I've told Chris all about it and—" She turned to Martha. "You don't have a part for a paramedic in here, do you? I bet Chris would say yes in a second!"

"*That* is a great idea!" Martha's eyes rounded. "Why didn't I think of it? Ooh – what about Mitch, Lauren? He could play one of the not so hot shots and—"

"I don't think so," Lauren said hastily. "Mitch is very serious about his career."

"So is Jesse," Pru added quickly.

"Mitch is impressed with what you're doing," Lauren continued, "but—"

"I get you." Martha nodded. "I guess it's the same with Jesse." She glanced at Pru. "Well, pooh."

"If I may make a suggestion," Tandy started. "I have a friend who might be interested in coming down here and helping us out. His name is Brock Thornhurst and he's waiting for his next role at the moment. So he should be free to come down here and—"

"Do we need to pay him?" Martha asked worriedly. "We all chipped in to pay you, but I don't know if everyone can stretch to pay another actor – not that it isn't a great idea," she ended hastily.

"No, no," Tandy assured her. "I think Brock will be intrigued enough to pay his own way here and will do it for free. If he had somewhere to stay."

"I bet Paul wouldn't mind giving him a free room at the motel," Martha replied instantly. "What do you think, Pru?"

"He might," she replied cautiously, aware that Paul was already giving Tandy a room for free, as a favor to Martha.

"That would be wonderful!" Tandy exclaimed. "I love my darling little room there, and I'm sure Brock would be happy with whatever is available."

"I'll call Paul." Martha reached for her phone which hid in her walker basket.

"Ruff!" Teddy stretched up and peered over Martha's lap as she pressed the buttons on the device.

"Hi, Paul," Martha began. "Yeah, she's here. I'm sure she loves it. She just called it darling." She winked at Tandy. "Uh-huh. Listen, do you have another room available? For free? Tandy wants to invite her acting friend down here to help us out with the lessons. You do? Hey, do you wanna be in my TV show? I can make you a nice motel owner – because you are – and you can help my retired lady detective out of a jam!"

Everyone was silent as they waited for Paul's reply.

"Goody!" Martha grinned. "Don't worry, I'll make you look real good. Okay. Uh-huh. Thanks, Paul. Bye."

"Well?" Tandy asked after a moment.

"He said your pal can stay for free too." Martha beamed. "And he can't wait to be in my show. So now I'll have to write a part in. Lemme see, which episode should that be?" She screwed up her eyes in thought.

"Perhaps if we start reading through the first episode, it might help you think of somewhere to put Paul," Tandy suggested.

"Yeah." Martha snapped open her eyes and nodded. "You must be used to writers doing this kind of creative thinking."

"I certainly have experienced it." Tandy smiled, and then looked at everyone. "Now, let's start reading the first page."

After thirty minutes, they took a break. Pru found herself in the kitchen, making coffee and hot chocolate. Luckily, Martha had laid in a good supply of the cocoa mix, because there would only be a few sachets left by the end of the evening.

Doris came to help, along with Lauren. They carried the mugs back into the living room, where Martha was regaling Tandy about her and Teddy's experience on a game show in LA.

"I heard about that, but I'm afraid I missed your episodes," Tandy said apologetically. "It sounds like it was a lot of fun."

"It was," Pru jumped in, smiling at Martha.

"Apart from the murder," Martha added. "But don't worry, we solved it."

"You did?" Tandy blinked.

"You mean you didn't hear about that bit, too?" Martha sounded disappointed. "It was even in the newspaper."

"The whole town read about it," Zoe added. "I saved a copy if you'd like to see it."

"I did too, but it's in my bedroom," Martha said.

"I'm sure there'll be time to look at it while I'm here," Tandy said. "Now, about tomorrow night. I can meet you at the church hall, if you give me directions."

"Oh, it's real easy to find." Martha proceeded to tell Tandy where to turn left and right from the motel for a few minutes.

Pru noticed Tandy furrowing her brow.

"Maybe it would be easier if you drove here, and then went over to the church hall following our car. Or you could ride with us."

"Yeah!" Martha nodded enthusiastically. "You can even ride in the front with Pru and I'll sit with Teddy in the back."

"Maybe that would be easier," Tandy accepted graciously.

After their hot cocoa break, they continued reading Martha's first episode. When they had nearly reached the end, Pru couldn't stop a yawn escaping.

"Sorry." She glanced around the room.

"Now you've got me going," Zoe said good-naturedly, before clapping her hand over a huge yawn.

"And me." Claire shook her head, trying to suppress hers.

"Maybe we should call it a night." Tandy looked over at Martha.

"Yeah, I guess so," Martha replied reluctantly.

"Tandy's had a long drive today," Pru reminded her.

"I forgot," Martha admitted apologetically. "Sorry. You look so fresh, even now." She looked at Tandy in admiration. "I think you're one of those people who always look well pulled together, like a – like a – fashion model!"

"Or a Hollywood actress!" Zoe giggled.

"Well, thank you." Tandy smiled. "I do try. You never know when a producer or agent will spot you at a restaurant or even doing something ordinary, like buying groceries at the supermarket. It's happened like that a couple of times – I've bumped into a producer who I worked with previously and who invited me to audition for a new project that my agent hadn't heard of yet. This was before I signed with Trish," she added hastily.

"And maybe if you weren't looking so smart he mightn't have offered you the chance." Martha nodded. "I get you."

Everyone rose and started saying goodbye to each other.

"See you tomorrow!" Zoe's brown eyes sparkled. "I can't wait to continue reading Martha's episode."

"Me neither," Doris agreed.

"Tomorrow night we'll start acting out some scenes," Tandy promised. She glanced at Martha. "I don't know if we'll have time to act out all your episodes but I'll give it a good try."

"Thanks." Martha nodded. "I knew you were the right choice when Trish suggested you. Yes, sirree."

CHAPTER 2

The next night, everyone turned up on time at the church hall. Tandy had arrived at Martha's house at the correct time, and they'd hopped into Pru's small silver SUV to make the short trip to the church hall, Martha in the back with Teddy as promised.

Pru reached for the old-fashioned key kept above the lintel of the wooden hall. The church itself was a cream clapboard affair, with stained glass windows, and dated back to the Gold-Rush era in the eighteen-hundreds.

"This is just charming," Tandy enthused, waiting for Pru to unlock the stout door.

"Everyone likes Gold Leaf Valley when they get here," Martha told her. "Don't they, Pru?"

"They seem to," she agreed.

"Pru's from Colorado, but she likes it here just as much," Martha boasted.

"I do," she confirmed.

She'd been here for just over a year now. Although she missed her parents and brothers, Martha and Teddy had also become part of her family, and now she'd made friends here with Doris, Lauren, Zoe, Claire, and Brooke. As well as Jesse.

They trooped into the large space. The wooden floorboards echoed under their feet.

"Ruff?" Teddy ambled over to where he usually sat next to Pru when she led the weekly yoga class. He also presided over the money tin.

"We're doing acting tonight," she told him. "Not yoga."

"And it's free this evening," Zoe added. "Sorry, Teddy."

"Wuff." Teddy looked disappointed.

"I bet you'll still have lots of fun helping us with our acting." Martha tried to cheer him up.

"Why don't we go over Teddy's part now?" Tandy suggested. She looked around the bare room. "Are there any chairs we can sit on?"

"Over there." Pru darted over and grabbed a few black plastic ones stacked against the wall. The others helped until everyone sat in a circle and looked expectantly at Tandy.

"Teddy has a part at the end of the episode, doesn't he?" Tandy asked.

"Yep," Martha replied proudly. "He's the retired lady detective's dog and she tells him all about her adventures when she gets home."

"I was thinking," Tandy said slowly, "it's a wonderful script already, Martha, but I think Teddy could be a real drawcard for your audience if he accompanied your retired lady detective on her adventures."

"Yeah!" Martha's eyes widened.

"Ruff!" Teddy sat up straight and looked excited.

"Like Inspector Rex," Pru said.

Everyone stared at her.

"It was an Austrian TV show about a police detective and his police dog, a German Shepherd. The Austrian title was Kommissar Rex. Then it turned into an Italian show with the same dog character but a different police detective, and now it's a Canadian show called Hudson and

Rex, but I haven't watched that series," she finished apologetically. She also thought it might be a bit longwinded to mention all the different actors who'd played the succession of police detectives in the show.

"You really do know stuff," Martha said in admiration. "That's because she's an assistant librarian," she told Tandy, "But one day she'll be the—"

"Head honcho of the whole Californian library system," everyone chorused.

Pru's cheeks flamed.

"You will," Doris said softly.

"Definitely!" Zoe asserted.

Everyone agreed, and Pru smiled. "Thanks."

"So, Martha, you're going to add Teddy into more scenes so he can accompany the retired lady detective on her investigations," Tandy confirmed.

"You betcha!"

"Wonderful. Now, why don't we try acting out the first scene? Martha, you're in the detective's office picking up some files you left behind when you retired a few weeks earlier and you hear those two not so hot shots discussing their new case. And Teddy is with you."

Martha nodded and tightened her grip on the script.

"Ruff!"

Everyone chuckled.

"And Zoe and Pru are the not so hot shots."

Pru focused on the lines she was about to say.

"Why don't we take it from—"

The stout hall door was suddenly flung open.

"Darling! I have arrived! But why are you stuck here in this dinky little backwater?"

A vision of glamour filled the doorway. Gently tousled strawberry blond hair framed a fifty-something face that looked well preserved, but Pru detected a slight hint of wrinkling, even under the expertly applied make-up. The woman wore a taupe cashmere wrap over a matching cashmere sweater, and white woolen slacks – possibly cashmere as well? Her feet were shod in gorgeous black ankle boots that looked like they cost a fortune.

"You're – you're—" Martha pointed at the stranger.

"Flora Forsey!" Zoe jumped up out of her seat. "I saw you in this old – older – movie a few months ago."

"Why, thank you, darling," Flora said in a posh, slightly British accent. Pru noticed her smile didn't reach her emerald green eyes. Her fingernails looked gorgeous – elegant long ovals in a pretty pale pink with a tiny sparkling crystal – or diamond? – subtly decorating each one.

"What are you doing here, Flora?" Tandy asked.

"I decided to join you here! You made it sound like such fun in your email. And, you did!" Flora stabbed a finger at Tandy. "You got a facelift, you sly old thing! Maybe that's why you got the glam grandma role instead of me!"

"You were up for the part as well?" Tandy frowned. "I didn't know that."

"I didn't want to say anything in case I jinxed it." Flora flounced toward their circle. "But it didn't matter, did it? Because you nabbed it instead!" There was a hint of humor in her voice, but Pru thought she detected an underlying note of envy.

"You got a facelift?" Martha stared at Tandy. "Wow. I couldn't even tell."

Pru thought when she'd first met Tandy that her skin had seemed particularly well rested for her age but Tandy had been so pleasant, and hearing about her life in Hollywood had been so interesting, that she hadn't thought any more about it.

"I had to confront reality." Tandy shrugged elegantly. "If I wanted to keep working, then I needed to look a little younger."

"And you succeeded spectacularly!" Flora enthused. "You must give me the name of your surgeon, darling."

"I will," Tandy promised after a moment. "But really, why are you here? You're not interested in giving some acting lessons, are you?"

"Don't." Flora shuddered dramatically. "That day I decided to help an old friend who was a teacher with her acting class …" She faced everyone. "Little children," she stage-whispered. "A nightmare! Never to be repeated!"

"We're not children." Martha frowned.

"Martha's written a wonderful TV show," Tandy said, "and has hired me to give them some acting lessons. Martha wants to make it herself."

Flora stared at Martha for a split second before shuddering again. "Darling, you don't know what you're getting yourself into," she began. "More experienced people have tried that and failed. Do you even have an agent?"

"She does," Pru replied.

"Yes, it's Trish," Tandy added.

"Trish?" Flora's eyes widened. "*Your* Trish?"

"I thought she was my Trish," Martha mumbled.

"And mine," Zoe piped up.

"Well, that is something." Flora shook her head. "That's one of the reasons I'm here, darling Tandy. I wondered if you'd put in the teensiest little good word for me with Trish? My agent Hal is retiring and I simply do not like his partner who is going to take over and run – or should that be ruin – everything." She placed her hand by the side of her mouth and whispered dramatically to Tandy, "And I don't think he likes me, either."

"Oh." Tandy blinked. "Well, yes, I guess I can ask Trish if she can meet with you."

"Splendid." Flora smiled. "One meeting will do the trick, I'm sure. Leave the rest to me."

There was a small silence as Flora looked expectantly at Tandy.

"Now?" Tandy asked.

"If you wouldn't mind?" Flora said hopefully.

Tandy plucked her black phone out of her elegant leather purse and dialed. After a quick conversation with Trish, she ended the call and turned to her friend.

"Trish says she can fit you in Wednesday next week at eleven a.m. at her office."

"Splendid." Flora smiled. "Thank you, darling."

"Now, we really must get started," Tandy said. "It's lovely to see you, but these ladies are paying me for acting lessons and I must deliver."

"Of course." Flora nodded. "But you wouldn't mind me staying, would you? I could give them a few pointers."

"I thought you didn't teach?" Zoe frowned.

"But I can make an exception. Since Tandy has just done me a favor." Flora smiled, but Pru wondered if it was genuine.

"Where were we?" Tandy studied her script. "Ah, yes. Martha, you're in the detective's office and you hear those two not so hot shots discussing their new case. And Teddy is with you."

"Teddy?" Flora looked around. "I don't see a man here and believe me, I'd know."

"Ruff!" Teddy replied.

Everyone laughed apart from Flora.

"This is Teddy." Martha patted her sidekick along his fluffy white shoulder. "He's my dog."

"And what a cutie," Flora said quickly.

Tandy turned their attention to the script, and they started reading their lines. Flora didn't interrupt until they had nearly finished the scene.

"Shouldn't you be saying it with a little more oomph, darling?" she asked Martha. "Like this. I don't think there'll be a case that I *can't* solve."

Martha glanced at Tandy.

"Say it the way you think it should be said, Martha," Tandy told her. "So we can see for ourselves." She shot a quick look at Flora.

"I don't think there'll be a case that I can't solve," Martha said seriously.

"I like it." Tandy nodded.

"Me too," Pru agreed.

"Yeah." Zoe added.

Everyone else murmured their approval, apart from Flora.

"I thought you were *teaching* them, darling, not just listening to them recite their lines."

"It's all part of the process," Tandy replied. "They haven't had the training *you've* had, Flora. Wasn't it RADA in England? And then—"

"Playing Juliet with the most marvelous, handsome actor as my Romeo," Flora reminisced. "Then Cleopatra, and so many other roles on the stage! Then I was lured to Hollywood – lured! – by a role in a movie and the rest as they say, is history."

Pru and Martha looked at each other. She wondered if Martha was thinking what she was thinking. Flora Forsey might have had bigger roles early on, but for a while now she'd been playing smaller and far less frequent parts in movies and TV shows. In fact, Pru thought that Tandy had been the more successful actress so far.

"Let's keep reading the script," Tandy suggested.

"Yes, let's!" Flora declared. She sauntered to the back of the room and pulled a chair off the stack, making a great show of carrying it all by herself back to the circle.

Tandy looked like she wanted to roll her eyes at the display but thought better of it.

Martha finished reading her scene, then looked expectantly at Tandy. "Well? Whatcha think?"

"I think you'll make a wonderful retired lady detective." Tandy smiled.

"Yeah!" Martha's eyes sparkled.

"Ruff?" Teddy asked hopefully.

"And you'll be a wonderful sidekick for Martha," Tandy told him.

"Ruff!" *Yeah!*

Everyone chuckled, even Flora.

They continued reading the script, Pru enjoying her role as one of the not so hot shot detectives, while Zoe read hers with a dramatic flair.

"Darling," Flora said when Zoe had finished telling off the retired lady detective, "have you ever thought of becoming an actress?"

"Not really," Zoe replied, although she looked pleased at the question, "but I did write a script for a princess movie and—"

"I knew it!" Flora jumped up from her plastic chair. "You're the Zoe Crenshaw who wrote the third princess movie!"

"I am." Zoe grinned.

"Now I see why Trish is your agent. Why aren't you writing these scripts instead of – instead of—" She looked at Martha as if trying to remember her name.

"Martha," Pru supplied.

"Yes, dear Martha."

"Because this is Martha's thing," Zoe replied simply. "And I'm glad I wrote the princess script but now I'm focusing on other things, like my pottery mugs, and trying out new recipes in my air fryer, and spending time with my husband."

"Zoe's mugs are very popular," Lauren stated.

"I think everyone in town has at least one in their collection," Brooke added.

"Oh, maybe I should take a look at them," Flora said, as if she were doing Zoe a favor.

"We've got a few on display at the café," Lauren said. "That's the Norwegian Forest Cat Café in town."

"Paul knows where it is," Zoe added. "If you're staying at the motel tonight."

Flora looked at Tandy. "Where *am* I staying, darling?"

"At the motel – if there's a vacancy," Tandy replied.

"What about a nice, cozy, bed and breakfast?" Flora asked hopefully. "I find them so much more welcoming than a *motel."* She made it sound as if a small-town motel was the lowest of the low.

"There aren't any," Claire spoke.

"Yeah, the motel is it now," Martha agreed. "And it's real nice. Why don't I call Paul and ask if he has a room for you?"

"That would be kind of you," Flora acquiesced.

"How did you get here?" Tandy asked her friend.

"I flew and then I rented this dinky little car, which is all they had left at Sacramento, and drove, darling, all the way here. Just over an hour!"

Martha dug out her phone from her walker basket, and in a few seconds started speaking to Paul. "Thanks, Paul." She ended the call and turned to Flora. "Paul says he's got a few rooms spare, which is good. He said he'll even give you a discount on account you're Tandy's friend."

"Marvelous!" Flora clapped her hands.

"You can follow me back to the motel when we finish here," Tandy promised. "Martha gave me a ride here, so you can follow us back to her house and then I'll show you how to get to the motel."

"You're too kind." Flora smiled, but Pru didn't think it reached her eyes again.

There was a *ping!* from Tandy's leather purse. "Excuse me." She delved into her bag and brought out her smart phone. "Oh, it's from Brock! He said he'll be here tomorrow night."

"Brock's coming? Why didn't you tell me?" Flora demanded. "I can't *wait* to see him!"

"I haven't had a chance," Tandy said wryly. "Besides, we're working right now, Flora – or trying to." She turned to Martha and the others. "I'm sorry, ladies, we haven't done as much tonight as I'd hoped for."

"No worries," Martha waved away her concern. "We've had a real good time, haven't we, everyone?"

"Yes," Doris said shyly.

"Yep." Zoe nodded.

"We can start earlier tomorrow night, if everyone can make it after work?" Tandy proposed.

"You betcha!" Martha grinned. "How about six-thirty, everyone?"

They all nodded.

"And I'm sure I can find the church hall on my own tomorrow," Tandy continued.

"I'll help you," Flora promised.

They started stacking the chairs and returning them to the back of the hall. Pru noticed that Flora didn't help; instead, she talked to Tandy in a low

46

voice. She wondered what it was about, but told herself it was none of her business.

"That was fun," Doris said to her as they finished putting the last chair on top of the stack.

"It was." Pru smiled. "I'm sorry we didn't get to your part in the script tonight."

"I'm a bit relieved," Doris admitted. "I thought I could do it, even though I was nervous with Tandy here, but now there's Flora too and …" she hesitated.

"What?" Pru urged in a whisper.

"I don't think she's as nice as Tandy."

CHAPTER 3

The next morning, Pru overslept and rushed through her breakfast. Instead of crunching away at her boring but fiber-rich cereal, she snatched a piece of raisin toast – with Martha's approval.

"I can't wait for this evening." Martha took a big bite of her toast, covered in butter. "I just hope we can make it through the rest of the episode. I want Doris to get her turn tonight."

"I'm sure she will," Pru replied.

"That's if Flora doesn't try to take over again," Martha added. "I don't know why she came all the way here. It's a bit strange if she only wanted Tandy to recommend her to Trish. Why didn't she call her instead?"

"Maybe she was feeling lonely?" Pru gulped down her last corner of toast.

"Maybe." Martha tapped a piece of toast against her plate. "Or maybe she heard rumors of Tandy's facelift and wanted to see it for herself!" She sat back in her kitchen chair with a satisfied smile on her face.

"Ruff!" Teddy agreed, sitting next to Martha's feet.

"You could be right." Pru scooted back her chair. "I've got to go or I'll be late."

"And Barbara doesn't like tardiness." Martha shooed her away. "Have a good day."

"You too."

"I'm gonna take Teddy to the senior center and tell them all about last night." Martha chuckled.

Pru hopped into her SUV and drove the short distance to the library. The January day was cold and wet, and she was glad she was using her car instead of attempting to walk.

She made it to the returns desk with three minutes to spare.

"Good morning, Pru." Barbara, her boss, and the director, nodded in her direction from the reference desk. "There's a stack of returned books for you to take care of and then I'll need to you set up the room for Greek conversation at eleven."

"Yes, Barbara." She eyed her boss's sharp brunette bob, and the elegant black suit teamed with a white shirt which featured a pussy cat bow. Barbara always looked immaculate, even at five p.m. when the library closed most days.

After turning on her computer, Pru took the first book off the pile and hit the barcode with the scanning gun. Then another, and another, the only sound in the large room the quiet beep of the scanner.

Then she stacked all the marked off books onto the trolley and wheeled it to the romance section, where she proceeded to shelve a third of the returns.

"Hi." An attractive male voice snagged her attention. She turned her head to see a tall man wearing dark slacks and a blue button-down shirt, with a rugged, good-looking face and short, wavy dark hair.

Jesse.

"Hi." She smiled back at him, her heart fluttering.

"How was last night?"

She'd texted him before she turned off her bedside lamp, telling him about Flora Forsey turning up unexpectedly.

"It was interesting."

"I'm sorry I've had to work late recently," he continued. "We've had some extra paperwork to handle, and Mitch wants to make sure those Christmas burglars stay behind bars."

"I understand."

"Do you need any help with your lines? I could come over and—"

"I'm reading one of the not so hot shot characters for the first episode. Martha suggested you read the part instead, with Mitch as the other not so hot detective, but Lauren and I both said no."

"You did?"

"You know Martha. If you read the part to help us out, the next thing she'd do would be to suggest that you play the part in her TV show." She paused. "Unless you want to?"

He shook his head, his lips quirking up. "If I wasn't already a police detective I might have said yes. But it's not going to be a good look for me since I really am one."

"That's what I thought." She smiled, glad that she'd read him correctly.

"Pru?" Barbara's voice floated from the reference desk. "Have you finished shelving those books?"

"I was just returning my novel," Jesse said easily, turning to face her boss across the room. He held up the book that had been under his arm.

"Oh, well, all right then, Jesse." Barbara settled back in her chair. "But I need Pru to complete her work as I'll have other tasks for her."

"Of course." He turned back to her.

"Another friend of Tandy's is expected tonight," she murmured quickly. "We're meeting at the church hall at six-thirty."

"It's tempting, but maybe I should stay off Martha's radar. I don't want to disappoint her if she asks me to play one of the detectives."

"I understand."

Jesse smiled goodbye, then strode to the exit, his phone buzzing as he did so. He answered, Pru catching him say, "Mitch," and then he was out of sight.

She quickly returned the books to the shelves, then got the room ready for Greek conversation, dragging the tables into a horseshoe shape.

The rest of the day passed smoothly, and she was able to finish all the tasks Barbara allotted her in record time. When the hands of the clock on the wall hit four, she shut down her computer and zipped up her handbag.

"Bye, Barbara." She sketched a wave.

"Good work today, Pru." Barbara was still at the reference desk. "I hear you had an unexpected visitor last night at your script reading group."

Pru's eyes widened. "How did you know?"

"A library director hears lots of things. Have fun tonight."

"Thank you." Pru smiled, then headed to the exit. She and Martha would have plenty of time to eat an early dinner before heading to the church hall with Teddy. She wondered if Barbara had heard about Brock arriving tonight.

***

After a quick dinner of left-over chicken stew, Pru drove Martha and Teddy to the church hall.

"I can't wait to meet this friend of Tandy's," Martha said. "It's gonna be a real fun night, isn't it, Teddy?" She swiveled around in her seat to wink at the fluffy white dog, sitting up straight in his own special car seat.

"Ruff!" Teddy parted his lips in a doggy grin.

Pru parked in the church parking lot, right near the hall. They were the first ones there, and she reached for the key kept above the lintel, unlocking the door with a metallic clink.

"Why don't I set the chairs up in a circle?" she suggested as Martha and Teddy followed her in, the wooden floorboards squeaking as Teddy trotted around the large room.

"Good idea." Martha sat down on her walker seat for a moment.

"Hi." Doris arrived a minute later, her hair looking a little disheveled. "I had to fill in for someone at the last minute today but I told Gary I had to leave just before six-thirty and he was good about it."

"I'm glad you're here." Pru smiled at her. "I was just setting the chairs up to save time for when everyone arrives."

"Let me help." Doris picked up a black plastic chair from the stack at the rear of the room and then another, carrying both towards Martha.

"I'm looking forward to your part tonight, Doris," Martha said. "And Tandy's friend Brock should be here as well. I can't believe I've already got two Hollywood stars helping us out with our acting lessons, plus Brock."

Pru thought maybe the word *star* was a little stretch, especially when it came to Flora's career, but she hadn't had time today to check out the actress's previous work. She'd wanted to run an internet search but she'd been busy all day at the library, and during her lunchbreak she'd spent part of the time in a brisk walk in the chilly weather, which she'd found invigorating and a welcome break from looking at the computer screen or her phone.

"Do you think Flora will turn up tonight?" Doris's face flushed.

"She made it sound like she would," Martha replied with a grin.

"Darlings, we're here!" Flora struck a dramatic pose in the doorway a minute later.

"Ruff!" Teddy wagged his tail at the newcomer.

"I'm sorry we're a few minutes late," Tandy apologized, coming in after her friend. She looked attractive and elegant in beige slacks and a soft blue sweater.

"We're waiting for Lauren, Zoe, Brooke, and Claire," Pru said.

"We're here!" Zoe called out behind Tandy, Lauren by her side.

"Sorry." Brooke rushed in a few minutes later. "I had a client come in insisting I give her a blow-dry for a last-minute date tonight." She shook her head. "I should have refused but she said she was desperate."

"For the date or the blow out?" Flora winked. "Maybe I should visit your salon while I'm here." She ran a hand through her artistically tousled waves.

"I think your hair looks great," Brooke replied.

"So does yours, darling." Flora inspected Brooke's chestnut hair with an experienced eye. "I love your cut."

"Thanks." Brooke smiled.

"Have you started?" Claire dashed in. "Molly wanted to come with me but I had to explain it wasn't her thing."

"Everyone's here now," Martha beamed. "Why don't we get going? I think we're nearly up to Doris's part."

"Yes." Tandy reached in her black tote bag and pulled out her copy of the script. "But before we begin reading, my friend Brock should be here any minute. He's already arrived at the motel but he wanted to freshen up before he got here."

"Will he find the way?" Martha asked.

"He's got GPS and Paul said he'd give him directions," Tandy replied.

"If he can find his way through the streets of New York, he can find his way here," Flora put in.

"New York?" Doris asked with interest. "Is he a stage actor?"

"At some point," Flora replied. "Now he's like the rest of us, hoping that his next audition will lead to something big in Hollywood."

"Forgive me, Tandy." A deep baritone voice reached their ears. A man of medium height opened the stout door and filled the entrance. Dressed in a long, black woolen coat over smart gray trousers and a white shirt, he wore slightly faded good looks and appeared to be in his late forties.

"I took a wrong turn at Oak Street," he continued.

Martha and Pru glanced at each other. Oak Street was one of the roads the Christmas burglars had targeted.

"You're here now, and that's what matters." Tandy smiled at him. "Thanks for doing this for me – and Martha. Everyone, this is Brock Thornhurst."

"Flora, what are you doing here?" Brock looked at her in surprise, but Pru wondered if he already knew Flora would be there. Perhaps he'd bumped into her at the motel earlier this evening?

"I wanted to see Tandy." Flora was sitting next to the actress, and placed an arm around her shoulder. "I missed her."

"Fabulous work, Tand." Brock inspected her face with a keen eye. "You must give me the name of your surgeon in case I need him one day."

"He is a she." Tandy smiled. "And she's supposed to be so good you can't even tell I had something done."

59

"She's done an excellent job," Brock assured her. "Hasn't she, Flora?"

"Yes," Flora agreed. "But we're in the biz, and we know what to look for."

"I couldn't tell," Martha put in.

"Thank you." Tandy looked at her gratefully.

"What are we doing?" Brock rubbed his hands together and looked around the circle.

"Let me get you a chair." Pru jumped up and hurried to the rear.

"Who's playing the male characters?" Brock asked.

"Me and Pru." Zoe answered.

"I can see why you asked me to come down here," Brock said to Tandy in an aside.

Pru placed the chair next to him with a smile.

"Thank you – Pru." He returned her smile.

His good looks were more noticeable when he smiled.

"I – I saw you on TV a few months ago," Doris started. "In a TV movie about a young boy looking for hidden treasure and you played his father."

"Ah, yes, that movie." Brock nodded. "What did you think?"

"I thought you were the best actor in it." Doris blushed.

"Thank you." He sounded sincere. "Now – Doris – which part are you playing tonight?"

"The waitress in the restaurant," she replied shyly. "I work at Gary's Burger Diner in real life."

"That's why I thought it would be good to write that role for her," Martha jumped in. "Since she has real life experience."

"Write what you know." Brock nodded. "Or in this case, play what you know. I like it."

"Let's get started." Tandy held up her script. "Now, when we stopped last night, we were up to the scene where Martha and Teddy drive off in their car to follow a clue."

"And that clue leads us to the restaurant where Doris works," Martha added eagerly.

"Is Teddy going into the restaurant?" Flora frowned.

"Yes," Martha replied.

"Darling, should it be written like that? Because—"

"Flora." Tandy's voice was no-nonsense. "Let's just read what's in the script for now."

They settled down to reading out the lines Martha had written. Pru had to hand it to her roomie – she definitely had a gift for writing realistic dialogue.

"Now, Doris," Tandy said. "This is where you come in and help Martha and Teddy. A dangerous looking man has just threatened her – he sat down at her table and told her to stop pursuing this case because he doesn't want something to happen to her. And he gestures to a table nearby – where there are four men wearing jackets, but they look like they could be hired muscle for him." She turned to Martha. "What does your retired lady detective do next?"

"She looks around the room and scans it for escape routes," Martha replied promptly. "But it's real tricky, because there are a ton of diners there, and there's only a narrow hallway leading to the kitchen."

"What about the rest rooms?" Flora interrupted.

"Poop, I forgot to put those in." Martha frowned.

"Never mind," Tandy said hastily, giving Flora a warning look. "I'm sure you can fix that bit up later on – if you want to. It's your script."

"Is this where I say my lines?" Doris asked hopefully.

"You do." Brock nodded. Martha had given him a copy of the script before they'd gotten started.

"Yeah, you're the waitress, and you can see that something's going down at my table, and you think I look like a nice older lady and you want to help. Because you're like that. So you come over and ask if I'm ready to order, and you knock my glass of water on the table and it trickles across to the bad man and he jumps up and that's my cue for me and Teddy to skedaddle!"

"What is Teddy doing while all this is going on?" Flora wanted to know. "Wouldn't he be growling at this bad man as you call him and—"

"Teddy is a last-minute addition on account of he was just going to wait for me at home and hear about all my adventures each night," Martha said, glancing down at him by her walker. "But I think Tandy's right, and he should be helping me catch the bad guys like he does in real life."

"Ruff!" Teddy wagged his tail hard.

"Catching bad guys in real life?" Brock frowned. "What do you mean?"

"I'm the president of the senior sleuthing club," Martha replied proudly. "Teddy and Pru are my members. And we've caught eight killers so far!"

"Martha, Teddy, and Pru were in the newspaper recently when they solved a case in LA," Lauren spoke. "And they help my husband Mitch at times." She turned to Martha. "Mitch and Jesse have to work late tonight, so Mitch wouldn't be able to come, even if he wanted to."

Martha nodded.

"Surely you're kidding." Brock stared at Martha. "You and your little dog Teddy?"

"And me," Pru spoke up for herself.

"Yeah, Pru is a major player in my club." Martha beamed. "She's real smart. And ethical. And Teddy likes catching the bad guys – or gals – and jumping on them and sitting on them until Mitch – or Jesse – can slap the handcuffs on them."

"Mitch and Jesse are the police?" Brock pursued.

"They're detectives," Lauren informed him. "Mitch is my husband and the head detective for Gold Leaf Valley. He and Jesse go way back to their Sacramento days."

"That's very interesting." Brock rubbed his slightly stubbled chin. "Maybe I should meet them. I've got an audition coming up to play a good cop and some real-life inspiration would be very valuable."

"We can talk about that later," Tandy told him. "We do need to finish reading this script tonight. I'm only here for a week and I want to get as much done as I can."

"Of course, darling," Flora nodded. "Let's go."

Tandy shot her a frustrated look, then talked Doris through the scene.

Doris tightened her grip on her script and opened her mouth to speak. "Oh – sorry, sir. Look what I've done! Oh dear." She looked up at Tandy.

"Very good." Tandy nodded in approval. "Oh – who is going to play this bad guy?"

"I will." Brock's voice changed as he snarled, "You stupid girl. This suit cost a fortune! My dry cleaning is going to come out of your tips – and it's going to take you a very long time to earn that much!"

There was a short silence.

"Wow," Zoe breathed. "That was amazing!"

Doris looked a little shaken but nodded her head in agreement.

"I have no idea why you're not having a big box office hit right now," Flora said.

"That was perfect," Tandy agreed. She turned to Martha. "What do you think?"

"Yeah, he was real good," Martha's eyes widened. "Hey, do you wanna be in that episode, Brock? If we can crowdfund enough money we could pay you properly – I think."

"You're making this yourself?" Brock sounded intrigued.

"Didn't I mention that when I asked you to come down here?" Tandy questioned.

"No, only that you needed a man for your acting lessons," he replied. "Tell me more, Martha." He looked at her with interest.

"Later, Brock," Tandy said briskly. "Let's continue with the scene. Doris, you apologize to Brock's character."

Doris did so, sounding very convincing as the scared waitress. Brock's character left to use the restroom, and that was Martha's cue to skedaddle through the kitchen, Doris leading the way.

"And Teddy," Tandy instructed, "you stay by Martha's side when she sneaks down the hallway to the kitchen, so nobody notices you."

Teddy dipped his head in a little nod.

"I've just had a thought." Flora frowned but no lines creased her forehead. "If Martha is going to play this retired lady detective character, what about her walker? Do you use it to get around everywhere?"

"Shoot." Martha pouted. "My retired lady detective doesn't use a walker, that's for sure. I can get by without it though, if I need to." She turned to Pru. "Can't I?"

"You can," she agreed, thinking back to the times when Martha had managed perfectly fine without it for a few minutes – usually when she wanted to do something a little dangerous, like climbing over a fence to spy on a neighbor.

"That solves that," Tandy said in satisfaction, flipping over to the next page in the script. "Martha escapes from the restaurant, and Brock's character is still in the restroom. His hired goons remain at the table because they've been trained not to go anywhere until Brock tells them to."

"And I find out something when I'm in the restaurant," Martha said.

"And that something leads you to catch the criminal," Tandy finished. "Let's do that scene."

"And then I get to show up those not so hot shots," Martha added with a big grin. "Yeah!"

Pru and Zoe exchanged amused glances.

They read through the rest of the script.

"Wonderful, everyone." Flora clapped at the end. "Brock, wouldn't it be something if you did play that bad guy? Did you know Trish is Martha's agent?"

"She is?" Brock looked at Martha with new respect.

"I think this TV series can really go somewhere," Tandy said encouragingly.

"And I have a meeting with Trish next week," Flora boasted. "Tandy set it up for me."

"I'm looking for a new agent," Brock said. "How about it, Tand?"

"I haven't been signed with Trish for long," Tandy replied. "I don't want to ask for too much too soon."

"But you've landed the starring role in this sitcom pilot," Flora reminded her. "Surely Trish would be grateful to you for recommending another actor? It's not as if Brock doesn't get any work."

"Thanks." He sounded a tad sarcastic. "I could say the same about you, Flor."

Tandy held up a hand and her friends fell silent.

"We're here to coach Martha and her friends," she reminded them.

"Doris, I must apologize." Brock turned his full attention to her. "I hope you'll forgive me for sounding so convincing in that scene. I fear I may have frightened you a little."

"I understand." A blush rose to Doris's cheeks. "You were acting."

"I think you have a lot of promise," Brock told her.

Doris's blush deepened.

"And Doris, you were very convincing, especially after Brock delivered those lines," Tandy said.

"See?" Martha grinned at Doris. "I knew you were gonna be good in that role."

"Thanks." Doris sounded pleased.

"Now, does anyone have any questions about this episode?" Tandy asked. "And then we can start on the next one. I have to get back to LA by next Monday night because I need to meet with the pilot producers on Tuesday, so I thought the best thing to do is to get through as many episodes as we can while I'm here."

Everyone murmured that was a good idea.

Nobody had any questions, so they moved on to the next episode. Pru played a yoga teacher and helped Martha out of a tight spot.

By nine o'clock, they were halfway through that episode, when Pru noticed Martha fighting off a yawn.

"Perhaps we should stop here," she said when it was her line. "And pick it up tomorrow night?" She hoped she sounded tactful.

"Good idea." Zoe nodded vigorously. "Lauren and I have to get up early to open the café."

"And bake the cupcakes," Lauren added.

"Ooh, what flavors?" Martha asked eagerly.

"Lavender, and salted caramel."

"I'll stop in and get some for me and Pru," Martha said.

"Ruff!" Teddy added eagerly.

Everyone laughed.

"That's right," Flora said. "Zoe makes pottery mugs. I must visit your café and take a look."

"You're welcome anytime," Lauren replied.

"I'll come with you," Brock proposed. "After all, we're staying at the same place." He turned to Tandy. "Thanks for arranging my stay for free. That helps me out right now."

"*You're* staying for *free*?" Flora's eyes widened. "Really? I have to pay!"

"I don't think Paul can stretch to everyone staying for free," Martha told them. "And I'd already arranged Tandy's stay with him. And then Brock was coming, but we didn't know about you."

"Not until you turned up," Claire spoke.

"Brock and I can manage things here if you need to go back to LA," Tandy added.

"Of course we can," Brock assured Flora.

Flora pouted. "You mean you don't want me here?"

"I didn't say that," Tandy replied quickly.

"It's fun having you here with us," Brock added.

"Why don't we pack up?" Tandy suggested.

Everyone assented and Pru started stacking the black plastic chairs, Lauren and Zoe helping.

She noticed Flora flouncing toward a back corner, and Brock following. They spoke in low tones, and then Flora's voice rose.

"I can't believe you get a freebie at the motel." She planted her hands on her hips. "It's not fair. I came here to support Tandy – I didn't even need to be asked! – and yet again, you get the good stuff instead of me!"

Brock said something to her that Pru couldn't catch. She looked at Lauren and Zoe, who both nodded at her, Lauren's eyes wide.

After Pru stacked the last chair, she turned toward the front of the hall, Lauren, and Zoe by her side. They walked past Flora and Brock, who were still talking.

"And what about Doris?" Flora demanded. "You were laying it on a bit thick, weren't you?"

"What?" Brock gave a half laugh. "The poor woman looked scared out of her mind after I delivered my lines. I was only being a decent human being. Besides, a little kindness to a plain woman never hurts."

Pru blinked. Had she really heard that? She glanced around the room, but Doris was talking to Tandy and

Martha near the door. Thank goodness.

Zoe had a *I can't believe you said that and I'm going to tell you off* look on her face, but Lauren touched her cousin's arm and shook her head.

Pru urged them towards Martha and the others, and with a steaming look in Brock's direction which he was oblivious to, Zoe joined them, scowling.

"Same time tomorrow night?" Tandy suggested, not looking tired at all.

"You betcha!" Martha grinned. "That's if it's okay with everyone else."

Every chorused a yes, and started saying their goodbyes.

"Tand!" Brock loped up to her, leaving Flora at the rear of the hall. "I'd really love an introduction to Trish. And …"

"And?" Tandy asked a touch warily.

"How about a role in your new sitcom?"

"What?" Tandy blinked.

"Come on, everyone knows this is going to be your big comeback, especially with the work you've had done on your face. All you have to do is suggest to the producers that you'd love it if your old friend Brock could be the leading male. You know we play well off each other."

"We do," she agreed after a second. "But that's a lot to ask. We haven't even shot the pilot yet. If it does well and they want to keep me in the lead role, then maybe I can, especially if they recast some of the other parts. But you can't expect me to ask them right now."

"You could if you really wanted to," Brock insisted. "Remember when you were desperate and begged me for a role in my TV movie? I went out on a limb for you then."

"And I told you I was very grateful." A slight hint of pink stained Tandy's cheeks. "And when my finances improved I bought you that gold watch you're wearing." She looked pointedly at his strong wrist – a handsome gold-faced watch graced it.

"And now *I* need a little help," he told her. "I paid my own way here to assist you with your little acting lessons and—"

"Okay, I'll talk to Trish," Tandy broke in. "But that's all I'm willing to do right now. Wait until the pilot gets picked up – *if* it gets picked up. You know nothing is certain in Hollywood."

"Darling, I think we can all agree on that." Flora sauntered toward them, a drawl in her voice.

"Are you going to be okay getting back to the motel?" Martha wanted to know. "Otherwise me and Pru can lead the way."

"We'll be fine." Tandy smiled, but Pru thought she looked distracted.

Everyone said goodbye, and Pru locked up once the hall was empty.

Tandy said goodbye to Martha and Pru, bending down to pet Teddy along his shoulder.

"How is it you're so nice and natural and polite?" Martha asked curiously. "That's not exactly how

Flora and Brock are. Don't get me wrong, I'm grateful they're helping us out too, but—"

"That's a nice compliment." Tandy smiled slightly. "But I'm afraid I've done some things in the past that I'm not proud of." She hesitated. "Sometimes I wish I could go back and change things, but if I could, then I mightn't be where I am now. I just hope that this pilot gets picked up and is a success. Then maybe I can make amends for the past." Guilt and sorrow shadowed her face.

"Well, *I* think you're a good person," Martha told her. "And you've made our day, coming down here to teach us how to act and go through the scripts with us. I know we all appreciate it."

"Thank you, Martha. I appreciate you too – and everyone in your group. You've made me, as well as Flora and Brock, feel very welcome."

Tandy waved goodbye and elegantly slid into her vehicle, her engine catching smoothly and yellow headlights lighting the way in front of her.

Martha turned to Pru. "I'm so glad Trish recommended her for our acting lessons. Aren't you?"

"I am," she agreed.

"And Tandy's not stuck up at all. Not like those other two!"

CHAPTER 4

"Where's Tandy?" Martha frowned the next night.

"I hope she's okay," Pru said.

Everyone was gathered in the church hall, awaiting Tandy's arrival. Even Flora and Brock were there.

"I'll call her." Flora took out her gold encrusted phone and pressed the buttons with her thumbs and forefingers, her delicate pink fingernails showing off their immaculate manicure, a tiny crystal in each one. "It's gone straight to voice mail – again."

"Maybe she doesn't want to answer your call." Brock dug out his own black phone from his coat pocket. "Let me try." A moment later, he shook his head, staring at the screen. "Voicemail too."

"I'll try." Martha reached into her walker basket and took out her phone. "If Teddy were here he could grab it for me, but he was real tired out tonight. We visited Lauren, Zoe, and Annie at the café on the way back from the senior center."

"Huh. No answer. Poop." Martha placed her phone on the walker seat.

"Maybe she got a phone call from Trish about bad news about the pilot," Flora suggested.

Pru glanced at her. It sounded like Flora wasn't that concerned if it *was* bad news.

"I hope not," Brock murmured. "She was going to put in a good word for me with Trish, like she did for you."

"Why don't we get started?" Flora suggested. "Brock and I can run lines with everyone."

"Shouldn't we check Tandy is okay?" Lauren ventured.

"Yeah, maybe she's having car trouble or something," Zoe added. "We should split up and go look for her."

"That's a great idea." Martha pointed at Zoe. "Yep, that's what we'll do."

"When is the last time anyone saw Tandy today?" Pru asked.

"At lunchtime," Flora answered. "I saw her in that burger joint, sitting at a table next to the window with the owner of the motel."

"Paul?" Pru asked.

"If that's his name." Flora shrugged. "He was tall and lanky and ordinary."

"They were," Doris confirmed. "I was working in the kitchen when Cindy the waitress told me Paul was with a glamorous woman and was it our acting coach, so I took a peek and told her it was Tandy."

"Good thinking," Martha praised.

Doris looked pleased.

"We should check with Paul," Pru decided.

"And that's why you're a member of my senior sleuthing club," Martha said in approval. "I'll call him." She proceeded to do so. "Hey, Paul, have you seen Tandy tonight? No? Yeah, we know you had lunch with her at Gary's. You haven't? Uh huh. Okay. Thanks." She ended the call.

"Well," she held their attention, "Paul had lunch with her at Gary's, but then didn't see her again this afternoon. But, he did see her car drive out of the motel lot about six-twenty this evening."

"So she must have been on her way here," Pru surmised.

"It looks like it." Martha nodded.

"We'd better go and retrace her route and check her car hasn't broken down or something." Zoe zipped to her feet.

"You and Lauren go to Oak Street – remember Brock said he took a wrong turn there on the way to here?" Martha turned to the actor for confirmation.

"That's right." He nodded. "I still can't believe I got swung around like that."

"Maybe that's what Tandy did," Martha said. "Pru and I will drive down the road to see if she's there – maybe she's stuck in a ditch or something. It did rain a bit today."

"Claire and I can drive back to the motel," Brooke offered. "In case Tandy forgot something and went back to get it. Maybe she got a flat on the way back."

"Good one," Martha approved. "Doris, why don't you go with Lauren and Zoe? I think it's best that no one searches alone."

"Okay." Doris nodded.

"What about me? And Brock?" Flora demanded.

"You two should stay here since you don't know the area like we do. We don't want you getting lost."

***

"I don't like this," Martha fretted once she and Pru were in the small SUV. "It's not like Tandy to be late."

"No," she agreed. "I hope she's okay."

"Maybe you should call Jesse." Martha shot her a sideways glance as Pru drove out of the parking lot. "Maybe there's been a traffic hold up somewhere."

"Good idea." She pulled over to the curb and dialed. The night was velvety black apart from a sprinkling of stars, and the air was a little chilly – even in the dark cocoon of the car.

"There isn't? Okay. Thanks." She ended the call and turned to Martha. "Jesse said there haven't been any traffic incidents today."

"Let's drive down the road and take a look-see for Tandy."

Pru drove slowly down the deserted road. It wasn't busy at the best of times and there weren't any streetlights. Only a couple of houses spaced far apart from each other lined the street and there weren't even any sidewalks – just overgrown grass leading to the overgrown front gardens. She couldn't see that well in the gloom, even with her headlights on high.

"There!" Martha pointed at a dark car just around the corner. It was parked at the curb and the driver's door was ajar.

"Oh, no." Pru parked on the opposite side of the road. Like the previous street, this one was fairly deserted as well. A house sat further up the road, but its lights were off. Before it lay a small, empty field.

"Stay here – I'll go." Pru hopped out of the car.

"I'm coming!" Martha clambered out of the passenger seat.

"I'll get your walker."

"No time for that!" Martha started across the narrow dirt road, her hands out at her side for balance.

"Be careful." Pru rushed to her side, just in case.

"I'm fine." Martha waved away her concern. "I can do it."

"Okay, but …" her voice tailed off. A woman lay on the side of the road, Pru's headlights revealing who it was.

Tandy.

***

"She can't be dead!" Martha clambered down to the prone woman. "Wake up, Tandy! Do it!"

"I'll check for a pulse." Pru did so, but there was nothing. She studied Tandy's figure. Blood stained her blonde hair and the neck of her beige sweater.

"No! I don't believe it! Tandy was going to shoot the pilot in LA and be a big success again. She can't be dead!"

"I'm sorry." Pru wrapped an arm around Martha.

"I really liked her," Martha mumbled. "And I hired her to come out here and teach us acting. If I hadn't, she'd still be alive somewhere in Hollywood."

"We don't know that," Pru said, although even to herself it sounded trite. Martha could very well be right. "I'll call Mitch."

A few minutes later, both Mitch and Jesse arrived in separate cars.

"I came as soon as Mitch told me." Jesse strode over to them and took Pru's hand. They hadn't left Tandy. "Are you okay?"

"I think Martha is really affected by Tandy's death," she told him in a low tone, standing up. She blinked back sudden tears. "I think I am, too."

"I'm sorry." He wrapped his arms around her and she leaned into him. After pressing a kiss on her hair, he stepped back and studied her, a concerned look on his face. "Where are the others in the acting group?"

"Out looking for Tandy," she replied.

The paramedics arrived, Zoe's husband Chris jumping out and hurrying to the scene.

"I'm pretty sure she's gone," Pru told him in a shaky voice.

He nodded, but expertly performed all the necessary procedures to make certain. "You're right," he said somberly. "I'm sorry."

Mitch spoke to Martha in a low voice, kneeling by her side, then helping her to her feet.

"Don't worry, Martha, I'll do everything I can to catch the killer," Mitch said.

"So it is murder, and not an accident?" Martha asked.

"The ME will have to confirm it, but it looks like someone hit her over the head with a blunt object. Now we just have to find it." Mitch frowned.

"But who would do that? Tandy was a real nice person and she was helping us act out my TV show." She turned to Pru. "What am I gonna tell Trish?"

Pru hadn't thought of that. "I can call her."

"No. I asked Trish to find us someone and I hired Tandy," Martha said. "I've gotta be the one to give her the bad news."

"Why don't we wait until we get home?" she suggested gently.

"I think that's a good idea, Pru," Mitch said.

"Yes," Jesse spoke. "We'd better go to the church hall now and wait for everyone to get back."

"I'll ask the uniforms to start looking for the weapon," Mitch stated.

"What am I going to tell Paul?" Martha fretted. "She was staying at the motel."

"I'll tell him," Mitch replied. "Don't worry about that."

Martha nodded. "Thanks."

Jesse followed them back to the church hall.

"Are you okay?" Zoe asked when she spotted them. "Jesse, what are you doing here?"

He nodded at Zoe, then turned to Pru. "Is everyone here?"

She surveyed the small crowd looking anxiously at them.

"Yes."

"What is it? What's wrong?" Doris sounded worried. "Did you find Tandy?"

"I'm afraid so." Martha spoke heavily. "And she's dead."

CHAPTER 5

Everyone gathered around Pru and Martha. After Martha sat down heavily on her walker seat, Pru took over and told them how they'd discovered Tandy's body, her voice shaking a little.

"No!" Flora wailed, her eyes wide. "I can't believe it! Not Tandy!"

"Are you sure?" Brock demanded. "I should go and check it *is* Tandy. Maybe you've made a mistake."

"There's no mistake," Pru said sadly.

"Yeah, I wish there was," Martha mumbled.

"Mitch and I will put all our resources into catching who did this," Jesse vowed. "You have my word."

"And we all know we can count on Jesse." Martha straightened her spine. "And Mitch."

"Yes, you can," Lauren put in.

"What's going to happen here?" Flora waved a hand indicating the church hall. "I came down here to visit Tandy, but now she's gone …"

"You and Brock will need to stay in Gold Leaf Valley for now," Jesse said, "until we tell you otherwise."

"How long will that be?" Flora asked. "I have a meeting in Hollywood next week, with Tandy's agent."

"And I have an audition next week," Brock spoke.

"We'll try to clear you both as quickly as possible," Jesse said after a moment.

"Don't worry, Flor, everything will be okay." Brock wrapped an arm around her shoulders. "At least we're both staying at the same motel – safety in numbers."

"You mean …" Flora turned up her face to him. "You think the killer might strike again?" She drew in a breath. "What if it was a case of mistaken identity? And the killer was trying to murder *me*?"

"Why would you think that?" Jesse frowned.

"Because why would someone kill Tandy?" Flora asked. "Everyone adored her."

"Why would someone want to kill you?" Jesse pursued.

"Because I'm a successful actress," Flora replied. "Maybe it's a jealous rival or a past paramour, or even a stalker I didn't even know I had!"

"You might have to come down to the station tomorrow and give us some more information about that," Jesse told her.

"I'm happy to, darling." Flora glanced at him coquettishly.

"If it was a stalker, he wouldn't make a mistake like that, would he?" Martha sounded like her old self. "He'd know right away if it was you or Tandy."

"That's an interesting theory." Brock nodded. "It reminds me of a TV movie where I played the romantic lead and a middle-aged man was stalking my beautiful girlfriend."

"What happened?" Doris asked.

"I killed him."

There was a sudden intake of breath.

"It was all in the script," Brock assured them. "I didn't have to do that much with all the camera angles." He turned to Flora. "How *did* I do it? There have been so many roles over the years." He frowned, then his brow cleared. "Ah, yes, I strangled him before he could do the same to me."

"That's right." Flora nodded. "I remember that one. It was one of your first roles, wasn't it, darling?"

Brock and Flora started reminiscing, until Jesse's voice cut in.

"Are you two okay to drive back to the motel? Otherwise I can take you."

"We're fine," Brock replied quickly. "Aren't we, Flor?"

"I'll ride with you and pick up my car tomorrow," Flora answered. "As you said, safety in numbers."

"What about Martha's script?" Zoe asked.

"I've booked the church hall for the rest of the week," Pru added. "Should we cancel, or should we—"

"The show must go on," Martha said stoutly. "I think that's what Tandy would have wanted. Look at all the setbacks she must have experienced over the years, but she got Trish as her agent and she was going to shoot a pilot next week. She told me she hoped it would lead to the big time again. So if she could do that, we can carry on with our lessons." She turned to Jesse. "If that's okay with you and Mitch?"

"I think that's a good idea," Jesse replied after a moment.

Pru looked at him in slight surprise and he gave her a little nod.

"Hey, Flora and Brock, do you wanna be our teachers?" Martha invited.

"Darling, we'd be delighted. Wouldn't we?" Flora nudged Brock in the ribs.

"Yes, delighted," he murmured.

"Goody." Martha smiled but Pru didn't think it had her usual exuberance.

"It will help occupy your time while you're here in town," Jesse stated.

"Same time tomorrow?" Brooke ventured.

"Yeah." Martha nodded.

"Why not?" Flora shrugged.

"I've got to get back to the station," Jesse said. "I think you should all go home now and regroup here tomorrow night."

Everyone agreed.

Jesse stood by Pru's side as she locked the church hall and replaced the old-fashioned key on top of the lintel. Everyone else waited a few feet away, their breath forming shapes in the suddenly chilly air.

"If Flora and Brock are coaching you, we'll know where they are in the evenings," he murmured.

"Do you think one of them did it?" She glanced over her shoulder at the two actors, talking quietly to each other near Brock's dark car.

"They're definitely suspects," he replied. "And so is anyone else who was in the vicinity at the time."

"But why would someone want to kill Tandy?" Martha gripped her walker handles and trundled toward them. "If Flora was murdered, I could understand it. But Tandy? She was a real lady."

"Yet someone took the risk of killing her," Jesse said. "And it's my job to find out why."

***

"I know what Jesse said last night." Martha finished crunching her piece of raisin toast in the kitchen the next morning. "And he's a good detective, like Mitch. But I want to find Tandy's killer. I feel responsible for bringing her out here."

"I know." Pru had just finished her boring but fiber rich cereal and was about to head to the library. "I'm sorry Tandy's gone. I liked her too."

"If we continue our acting lessons, we can keep an eye on Brock and Flora," Martha added. "As well as get going with my scripts. Hey!" She clicked her fingers. "If my TV show ever gets made, I'm gonna dedicate the first episode to Tandy."

"I'm sure she would have liked that. How did the phone call go with Trish last night?"

When they'd returned home from the church hall, Martha had insisted on calling Trish and telling her the bad news. She'd also waved away Pru's offer of assistance, saying it was something she had to do herself. She'd said goodnight and taken her phone to the bedroom – with Teddy.

"Not great," Martha replied, her tone somber. "Trish was understanding – and real sad. She said she liked Tandy and was thrilled she'd landed the starring role in the pilot."

"Is she still going to take the meeting with Flora next week?"

"She said she would." Martha nodded. "And Trish is a woman of her word. But now Tandy's gone I don't know if she will take Flora on, but she said she'd see."

"What is Brock going to do?"

"Trish didn't mention him." Martha frowned. "So I don't know if Tandy spoke to her about having a meeting with him too. Remember she said she'd speak to Trish about him when Brock was pestering her about it?"

"It does seem suspicious that Tandy was killed when they were both in town," Pru remarked. "But why would either of them murder her? They both wanted her help to land Trish as their agent."

"It's a toughie, that's for sure," Martha agreed. "But that's why we're the senior sleuthing club – we crack tough cases all the time." She looked down at the side of her chair. "Don't we, Teddy?"

"Ruff!"

CHAPTER 6

During her lunchbreak that day, Jesse called Pru.

"We've found the murder weapon," he told her. "It was a tire iron."

"Where was it?" She sat at a table in the small breakroom, having just finished her ham sandwich. There was no one else around.

"In that empty field." He sighed. "It was covered in cow dung. We don't know if we'll get anything useable from it."

"At least you found it," she sympathized.

"The blood on it matches Tandy's," he continued. "We got a rush put on it. Since she was a celebrity, there'll be more interest in this case from the media. Even Thelma from *The Gold Leaf Valley Gazette* contacted the station today wanting to interview Mitch about it. Maybe she'll want to talk to Martha too."

"Probably," Pru agreed. "Thelma can be a real go-getter."

They chatted for a couple more minutes, then Jesse said he had to go. "Let me know if you have any problems at the church hall tonight. We'll be questioning Flora and Brock today. You should be okay, but…"

"I'm sure we'll be fine," Pru assured him. "Teddy will be there."

He chuckled. "Tell him hi from me."

***

That evening, everyone made a fuss of Teddy – apart from Flora.

"Where is she?" Martha asked Brock. "I thought you were both coming tonight. Is Flora okay?"

"I saw her this afternoon and she said she'd be here." He frowned. "I drove her back here this morning to pick up her car and we both had to visit the police station to give statements. I even waited for her after and we grabbed burgers at that joint. Then we went back to the motel." He pulled out his phone and dialed.

"Flor, are you okay? Everyone's waiting for you and—"

There was silence as Brock listened to her reply from the other end of the phone.

"Really? Of course I can handle things here, I'm not an amateur."

There was another silence.

Brock sighed. "All right. I'll see you when I get back to the motel." He ended the call.

"Well?" Martha demanded.

"I'm afraid Flora is not feeling up to it." He shook his head. "Tandy's death has hit her hard. She's begged off tonight – says she needs peace and quiet to gather her thoughts."

"That's a shame," Martha commiserated.

"Still." Brock surveyed the small group. "You've got me and I'm sure I can whip you all into shape. Now, where were we with the script? Was it still episode one or had we moved on to episode two?"

"We're halfway through episode two," Doris said shyly. "Pru plays the yoga instructor."

"Of course." Brock threw her a dazzling smile. "Thank you, darling Doris. Let's pick up where we left off the other night."

Zoe gave Brock a fuming glance as she flicked through her script.

Pru hadn't had time to tell Doris what she, Zoe, and Lauren had overheard the other night, when Brock had dismissed his charming manner with Doris when he spoke to Flora. But surely Doris had the right to know? Was Brock a player? Did he break hearts wherever he went? She didn't want Doris's heart to break.

Brock took them through the rest of the script but Pru couldn't help feeling it wasn't the same. He also gave Doris some attention, even though she didn't have a speaking role in that episode.

Teddy sat by Martha's side, and when Brock gave him his cue, he obliged each time.

"Martha, your dog really is something," Brock said when they'd finished reading the script. Without Flora there to interject periodically,

103

they'd finished in record time. "Maybe Trish should take him on as a client, too."

"That's what I was thinking." Martha sounded pleased. "I'll talk to Trish about it. Tandy suggested Teddy have a bigger part in the show and she was right. Just imagine if a big-time movie producer sees him in my show and offers him a big movie role!" Her eyes lit up.

"Tell me more about this crowdfunding idea," Brock pressed.

"Pru's gonna help me set it up," Martha replied. "Since I can't afford to make a TV show myself, even a little one, we're going to set up a page on one of those crowdfunding sites and ask people to chip in."

"You can give people rewards for donating," Zoe spoke. "They could be cast as an extra."

"Yeah!" Martha pointed a finger at her. "And what about a speaking role if they donate a ton?"

"What about your friends, Brock?" Lauren asked. "Would they be interested?"

"Yeah, they could donate money and buy themselves a speaking part. Then we'd get real live actors and it won't cost me – us – anything." Martha chuckled.

"That's certainly an idea." Brock rubbed his chin. "I don't know if my agent would agree to me working for free, though – or paying for a part. But I think you would get plenty of desperate thespians who would."

"Yeah!"

"Ruff!" *Yeah!*

Everyone laughed, even Brock.

"But even if you make this show," Brock continued, "how are you going to get it out there?"

"I'm gonna put it up on one of those video sites – or more than one," Martha answered promptly. "And then I'll make money from the ad breaks in it."

"You certainly have thought of everything." He eyed her with awe.

They agreed to start on episode three. Brock assigned Doris a small speaking part, as well as everyone else. He even took on the part of one of the not so hot shots instead of Pru, which she didn't mind. She found herself impressed by his acting, and wondered if he would have been more successful if he'd concentrated on playing bad guys instead of romantic leads.

When it was nine o'clock, Martha yawned. "Sorry, but I'm pooped."

"Wuff," Teddy added sleepily. He'd settled his head on his paws and looked like he wanted to go to bed.

"Why don't we pick it up tomorrow night?" Brock suggested. "Tomorrow is Saturday. Is everyone okay to come back on the weekend?"

There was a chorus of yeses.

He turned to Doris, who sat next to him. "You were great, Doris. Have you ever thought of acting as a career?"

"No." She smiled in a pleased manner. "I just work at Gary's."

"But you're far more than a restaurant worker," Brock expanded. "Maybe Martha can give you an extra role in her series, or have you in a recurring role as the waitress. The restaurant could be the retired lady detective's favorite and she goes there regularly, so when you see her in danger in the first episode, that's another reason why you want to help her."

"That's not a bad idea." Martha pointed at him. "I'll give that some thought and see if I can work it into the script. And he's right, Doris." She winked at her. "You're real good at playing the waitress in here." She tapped her script. "As well as the receptionist part tonight."

"Thanks." Doris flushed with pleasure.

"We'd better go home." Zoe rose and picked up her black plastic chair. She glanced at Pru and then gestured toward the rear of the hall where the unused chairs were stacked.

Pru nodded discreetly. She followed Zoe to the back, Lauren following with her chair.

"I don't trust this Brock guy," Zoe said in a fierce whisper when they reached the stack of chairs.

"Me neither," Lauren agreed. "He's too smooth. And I'm worried he's just amusing himself with Doris."

"I know what you mean," Pru told them. "I haven't had a chance to tell Doris what we overheard Brock say to Flora the other night, but I think I should."

"Definitely." Zoe nodded, her pixie bangs hitting her forehead.

"Do you need help?" Doris asked hesitantly, joining them with her chair.

"No, we're fine." Zoe flashed her a smile. "Let me take that for you."

"Thanks." Doris handed her the chair. "I'll see if Brooke and Claire need me." She rejoined the others who were talking to Martha.

Pru watched as Doris took Brock's chair without a word of protest from him, and then walked back to them, along with Claire and Brooke.

"I think I'm in episode four as the hairstylist," Brooke told them. "I'm looking forward to it."

"And Martha's written me as the soccer mom in episode five. Wouldn't it be great if Molly could be in it, too?"

"Why don't you ask Martha about that?" Pru asked.

"That is a great idea." Zoe grinned. "Molly is so cute. Maybe she and Teddy could have a scene together."

"Now *that* would be so cute!" Brooke exclaimed.

"It would." Claire hurried over to Martha and started speaking to her.

Martha's eyes widened and she grinned. She grabbed a pen out of her walker basket and started scribbling on the back of her script.

"I think Martha's TV show is going to be awesome!" Zoe held up her hand for a high five. The sound of palms gently hitting palms echoed throughout the hall.

***

"I'm gonna call Trish this morning," Martha announced the next day at breakfast.

"Does she work on the weekend?" Pru queried.

"Huh. Good question." Martha chewed a corner of her raisin toast. "I'll try her anyway and see."

"Is this about taking Teddy on as a client?" Pru smiled at the fluffy white dog, sitting next to Martha's kitchen chair.

"Yep," Martha replied proudly. "Brock was right – Teddy's so smart and cute he should have a Hollywood agent, especially since he's gonna be my co-star."

"Ruff!" Teddy wagged his tail so hard, Pru wondered if it would spin off and sail through the kitchen.

"I'll do it right now." Martha fished her phone out of her walker basket and dialed.

Pru crunched her boring cereal as quietly as she could, so she could hear the conversation – at least Martha's end of it.

"Trish!" Martha sounded as excited as she looked, pink spots of color on her face. "It's me, Martha. Do you wanna take Teddy on as a client? Now he's gonna be my co-star in my new show, Brock Thornhurst suggested that he should have an agent and—"

"Uh-huh. Uh-huh. Hmm. Yeah, I guess so. Okay. Yeah, it's going good apart from Tandy being killed." Martha's voice grew somber. "Okay. Yeah. I understand. Thanks. Bye."

"Well?" Although by the tone of the second half of the conversation, it didn't sound as if Teddy was going to be Trish's new client.

"She said it's a real interesting idea but maybe we should wait until I make the TV show and see how he acts in it. And then she'll watch the episodes and make a decision. But she did say she has first dibs on signing Teddy."

"That's something," Pru said. She'd met Trish a while ago and had liked the savvy young woman.

"Yeah. And I'd rather Trish be Teddy's agent than anyone else," Martha said. "So, what are we gonna do today? Tonight we're meeting everyone at the church hall again. But I don't know if Flora is gonna show up or not. It was nice of Brock to be there last night, but I think Tandy was a better acting coach."

"I know what you mean."

"Ruff," Teddy added soberly.

"I could take Teddy for a walk this morning," she offered.

"That would be great." Martha beamed. "I wanted to add Molly to the episode Claire is gonna be in like she suggested –Molly and Teddy together – it's gonna be so good!"

"Maybe you should be a TV producer for real," Pru teased in an admiring way.

"Who knows?" Martha shrugged happily. "I'm only in my seventies – anything could still happen!"

When Pru took Teddy out for a walk a few minutes later, she thought about her friend's words. She only hoped she had Martha's zest for life when she was that age.

Her eyes widened when she spotted Doris walking ahead toward the café.

"Come on, Teddy," she told him. "I need to speak to Doris!"

"Ruff!" He quickened his pace from a slow amble to almost a jog.

"Doris!" she called out, waving a hand in the air.

Doris turned and smiled when she recognized them, brushing a limp strand of hair off her brow. She wore faded jeans and a blue sweater.

"Hi, Pru. Hi, Teddy." She bent to pat him.

"Are you working today?" Pru asked.

"No, I've got the weekend off." Doris smiled. "I was just heading to the café."

"There's something I wanted to talk to you about." Now Pru felt awkward.

"What is it?" Doris asked curiously.

"Maybe we should go somewhere private."

"Now you really are intriguing me."

There was a small alcove between two small shop frontages.

"Why don't we duck in here?" Pru suggested.

"What is it?" Doris frowned.

"I don't know how to say this," she started, "but it's about Brock."

"What about him? He's great, isn't he?" There was a dreamy look on Doris's face.

"I don't think he's exactly what he appears to be."

"How do you mean?" The dreamy expression faded.

"I overheard him talking to Flora the other night – so did Zoe and Lauren."

"And?"

"And …" she hesitated. How could she say this tactfully and not hurt Doris's feelings? "I think he might be a bit of a player."

"A what?" Doris blinked.

"A player. You know. A guy who isn't sincere with women even though he pretends to be. And, he and Flora might have a romantic past."

"Really?" Doris furrowed her brow. "I didn't notice anything like that between them. I thought they were just good friends who worked in the same business."

"Yes, I think you're right there," she agreed, although she wondered exactly how good a friend Flora and Brock really were to each other. "But from what we overheard, it sounded like he might be amusing himself by flirting with you."

"Flirting?" Doris looked surprised. "I thought he was just being kind. I mean, we were sitting next to each other and he has a lot of acting experience. Why would he be interested in me?" She fingered a strand of her dishwater-colored hair and waved a hand down her blue sweater and faded jeans. "I mean, I'm not exactly red-carpet material, am I? Not like Flora or Tandy."

"Don't say that," Pru urged. "I – we – don't want you to get hurt, that's all. Brock will be going back to LA next week or as soon as Mitch decides he can leave town."

"Maybe I have been a little starstruck," Doris admitted after a moment. "But you can't blame me. He's a man who's been in TV movies and shows and on the stage, and now he's sitting right next to me in our church hall and telling me he thinks I've done a good job reading my lines. This is the most exciting thing that's happened to me for …" She closed her eyes, thinking. "Probably the *only* exciting thing that's ever really happened to me." She opened her eyes and looked directly at Pru.

"I hope there will be lots more fun and exciting things happening to you in the future." Sincerity rang in her voice.

"I've been working in the kitchen at Gary's for years and I rent a tiny apartment. I thought I was pretty content with my life, and then you moved to town and we became friends and I joined the book club, and reading books opened up my world. And now Brock Thornhurst has arrived, as well as Flora and Tandy …" her voice trailed off for a moment, "… and it really has been the most interesting thing I've experienced." She paused.

"But don't worry. I'm not totally naïve. Sure, I might daydream about Brock whisking me away to Hollywood and asking me to accompany him to a red-carpet event, but I know that's not going to happen.

Even if I got a makeover, I don't think I could ever compete with Flora's glamorous look."

"I think you're fine just the way you are," Pru said loyally. "And Flora might look glamorous, but she's probably expected to in her line of work. I'm not into wearing make-up and I don't miss it."

"But you don't need to," Doris protested. "Your auburn hair is gorgeous and you have a real fresh-faced look about you. I've hit forty and I'm not going to recapture my twenties, no matter how much make-up I could splash on my face – even if I knew how to apply it expertly." She chuckled wryly. "I thought I'd accepted that I would never turn heads, then Brock arrived and gave me some attention."

"I'm sorry," Pru replied awkwardly.

"Don't be. You're a true friend, not wanting me to get my feelings hurt. But I'm a big girl. And a bit more daydreaming about Brock won't do me any harm. Like you said, he'll be leaving next week, anyway."

They chatted for a few more minutes, Teddy stretching up against Doris's leg in a comforting manner.

"Thanks, Teddy." Doris scratched him behind the ear. "You and Pru will always be my friends."

After a moment, they said goodbye, Doris promising to be at the church hall that evening. "I wouldn't miss it." She smiled, then waved goodbye, heading down the street.

"Let's go home," Pru suggested to Teddy.

"Ruff."

She was glad she'd had the opportunity to talk to Doris, but she wished she hadn't felt the need to warn her friend off Brock. But if she'd been a coward, she would have felt even worse. She'd speak to Martha when she arrived home about her plans to give Doris a recurring role in the series – it would be something she was sure Doris would enjoy.

When they returned home, Martha was sitting on the sofa, a script in her hand.

"I've done it!" Martha grinned. "I've put little Molly in Claire's episode."

"Ruff!" Teddy wagged his tail.

"Yeah, Teddy, you're in it with her – and me, of course." Martha waved the pages in the air.

"What about Doris?" she asked. "Have you been able to give her a recurring part as the waitress?"

"Yep," Martha replied proudly. "Did it last night."

"That's great. I think Doris will be pleased."

"She's a good girl." Martha nodded. "Who knows? Maybe Brock is right and Doris could get work as a real actress one day! Hey! What if Trish sees Doris in my show and snaps her up?"

"That would be amazing."

"Wouldn't it? And what if Doris wins some kind of award one day? Do you think she'd thank me for giving her a start in the biz – and Trish of course?"

"That could definitely be possible."

"Yeah!"

Pru made tuna sandwiches for lunch, and then Martha announced they should visit the motel and speak to Paul, the owner.

"We've got our acting class tonight," she reminded her.

"I know, but I'm feeling good," Martha replied. "And we have to talk to Paul. He was one of the last people to see Tandy alive."

"You're right," she replied after a moment.

"Ruff!"

***

They set off in Pru's SUV to the motel, which was a short distance away. Gold Leaf Valley Motel was a Swiss chalet style building and had seen better days, but its fading glamor added a certain type of charm. Rose bushes adorned the front garden, along with a neat, green lawn. Although the building could use a coat of paint, Paul maintained the grounds nicely.

"I wonder if Flora will turn up tonight," Martha mused. "At least we got somewhere with the script yesterday without her interrupting all the time. I wonder – if she turns up tonight and Brock doesn't, will she interrupt herself?"

"That's an interesting thought." Pru hid a smile, parking in front of the office.

After retrieving Martha's walker from the trunk, they entered the small, neat office.

"Can I help – oh, hi, Martha." Paul looked up from the computer screen, his tall lanky frame dominating the desk. "Sorry, I thought you were a guest – or a potential one."

"No worries. We came to talk to you about Tandy," Martha declared.

"Tandy." He shook his head, suddenly sorrowful. "I still can't believe it."

"We heard you had lunch with her at Gary's Burger Diner," Martha prompted.

"That's right." He sighed. "I couldn't help myself – I've always admired her as an actress. I loved that sitcom she was in years ago, so when you asked me to give her a free room I couldn't believe it! And she was just as nice and gracious as I imagined she would be in real life. So I asked her out to lunch – just in a friendly way – and she accepted! She wasn't stuck up like her friend Flora seems to be – and she asked about me and my life here in Gold Leaf Valley. I was starting to think I could even ask her out on a real date, when her phone rang while we were finishing our burgers, and it was her agent checking in, and then I realized she was way out of my league and I'd been kidding myself."

"Well, maybe you were," Martha said thoughtfully. "And maybe you weren't. Who knows? Maybe Tandy would have said yes if you'd asked her out on a real date."

"I guess we'll never know." Paul sounded downcast.

"But you can rack your brains now and tell us if you noticed anything unusual on her last day here – even her second last day," Martha continued. "Since I'm the president of the senior sleuthing club, and I invited

Tandy down here, I'm taking a big interest in her case – even if I – we – have to catch the killer ourselves!"

"Ruff!" Teddy added.

Paul gave a small smile. "Mitch has asked me about that, too. And really, the only thing I can think of is that Tandy seemed a little surprised when her friend Flora arrived."

"What about when Brock arrived?" Pru asked.

"She was expecting him," Paul answered. "They seemed to get along okay. But sometimes Flora can be a bit dramatic. You should have heard her the first morning when she came to the breakfast room. First, she said she'd only have lemon water, but then when she saw the pancakes my other guests were helping themselves to, she asked for some. But then she complained that I didn't have sugar free syrup and she ended up eating them plain. By the way she acted, you would have thought she'd been forced to starve."

"That's interesting." Martha nodded. "But what about when Tandy set off for the church hall her last …" her voice faltered "… evening here?"

"I saw her car drive out from the window here." He pointed to the large window behind them. "When I'm sitting at my desk I can see out to the parking lot – that's if I glance up from the computer screen. But I didn't notice anything unusual. Not like another car following her out right away, but then the phone rang so I grabbed it."

"Huh." Martha sounded disappointed. "What about Flora and Brock?"

"I didn't see them leave. The person on the phone wanted to make a reservation but then they couldn't decide on the dates and the booking took a while. When I looked out of the window again, Flora's and Brock's cars were gone."

"Really?" Martha perked up.

"Yeah, they were walking past the office a couple of hours earlier. Tandy and I had returned from Gary's Burger Diner by then and I was in here doing paperwork – or maybe I should call it computer work. Anyway, I heard raised voices and I looked out the window to see what was going on. I was just about to get up and see if there was something wrong, when they'd disappeared. They must have kept walking all the way down to the end of the building and turned the corner."

"What were they saying?" Pru asked.

"Something like, '*I don't believe you*.' That was Flora. And Brock said, *"But I'm telling you the truth. Can't you see that? It wasn't my fault. I did everything I could to stop him, but I was too late."*'"

"Now that's real interesting." Martha nodded.

"It is," Pru agreed.

"Ruff!" Teddy stretched up his full-length against the counter and peered over it.

"You're a good detective, Teddy." Paul chuckled.

"Are Flora and Brock here now?" Martha waved a hand toward the parking lot. "Or have they gone out?"

"I didn't notice them leaving, but who knows?" Paul shrugged.

"Which rooms are they in?" Pru asked.

"Six and eight, on the ground floor."

"What about Tandy?" Martha wanted to know.

"She was in twelve – one of my best rooms." Paul's voice dropped.

"Is her stuff still in there?"

"For now." He nodded. "Mitch said to leave everything as it is until they finish in there. But I don't think they found anything interesting. If they did, they didn't mention it to me."

"Have Flora and Brock been interested in looking in Tandy's room?" Pru asked.

"Now that's a good one." Martha pointed a finger at her. "That's why you're in the senior sleuthing club."

"No." Paul shook his head. "Maybe they're just hiding it well, but I didn't think either of them were too broken up about her death. It's a real shame. She seemed a lovely lady and I know she was doing them both favors with asking her agent to take them on."

"How do you know that?" Martha's interest quickened.

"I heard the two of them talking about it – or maybe arguing is the right word. Right after she died, too." He tsked. "Brock was upset that Tandy died before she got him an appointment with her agent and Flora seemed to rub it in a bit that Tandy had already set up hers."

"That does sound like Flora," Martha replied. "Why don't we take a stroll around the grounds and see if we can find Flora and Brock?"

"You're more than welcome," Paul said. He hesitated, then lowered his voice, even though they were alone in the office. "If you want to take a peek in Tandy's room, I can give you the key."

"Thanks." Martha's eyes lit up. "We'll let you know about that."

"Is there anything else I can tell you?" he asked.

"Not right now." Martha screwed up her eyes in thought. "I'll get back to you about that as well."

"Anytime. Tandy was a lovely person – I hope you catch whoever did this."

"Me too," Martha vowed.

"Yes," Pru found herself saying. She meant it.

"Ruff!"

CHAPTER 7

"Ooh, look! There's Brock!" Martha barreled the walker toward him as if she were a racing car driver.

Brock stood stock still in the garden, staring at them, his eyes wide.

"Hey, Brock!" Martha was a little out of breath.

"For a moment there, I thought you were going to run me over with that thing." He tried to make light of it. "Hello, Pru."

"Hi."

"Ruff!" Teddy danced around him, Pru following him with the lead, then he settled down next to Martha.

"What are you doing here?" he asked.

"Investigating Tandy's death," Martha told him bluntly. "And I found out something real interesting."

There was a pause.

"What was that?" Brock realized that was his cue.

"You and Flora were overheard having a real interesting discussion." Martha turned her head this way and that, scanning the grounds. "Where is she, by the way?"

"Lying down. She said she needed to regroup and have a rest before she joins us at the church hall tonight."

"Someone told us you and Flora were having a discussion and she said she didn't believe you," Pru suddenly spoke. "And then you said, *But I'm telling you the truth. Can't you see that? It wasn't my fault. I did everything I could to stop him, but I was too late.*"

Brock took a step back in surprise. "How on earth did someone overhear us? Flora was helping me practice for my upcoming audition. We thought we'd go for a walk and run lines at the same time. I find it good for my creativity."

"So it was just reading from a script?" Martha sounded disappointed.

"No script." Brock's voice was a tad smug. "I've memorized my lines already, because I'm a professional. When you're making your TV show, Martha, and I sincerely hope you do, you and your charming cast will have to learn that skill as well."

Pru wondered if he meant to sound so patronizing.

"Was Flora reading from the script?" she asked.

"Yes," he admitted. "But I can't really expect her to memorize the other actor's lines, can I? Besides, she has an upcoming audition – or so she tells me – and is being a bit hush hush about it."

"Is that why she wants to get a new agent?" Pru found herself asking.

"You'd really have to ask her that," Brock replied, "but I think so. And she said her agent Hal is retiring, and since she doesn't like his partner, managing to get signed by an up-and-coming agent like Trish would be a coup for Flora."

"And what about you?" Martha quizzed. "You wanted Tandy to get you an introduction to Trish."

"You've got me there." Brock laid his hand on his heart. "I've been with my agent for a long time and I think he just doesn't have the same enthusiasm for the biz like he used to. And if Trish was my agent, it might get me renewed interest by casting directors."

"Did Tandy set that up for you?" Martha pressed.

"She didn't have time before she …" his voice dropped "… died."

"You mean she was murdered," Martha corrected him.

"Ruff," Teddy sounded sad.

"I was trying to be delicate." He sounded a little affronted. "After all, my mother raised me to be a gentleman."

"Where is she?" Pru found herself curious.

"Freezing in Montana right now, but she loves it there," he replied. "I can't convince her to come out and join me in LA, either. I try to visit her as much as I can but sometimes money's a bit tight."

"Yet you came to Gold Leaf Valley to help out Tandy for free," Martha said.

"That's right." He nodded. "Tandy was a good friend and we used to help each other out all the time. I was happy to visit her here and assist if I could. I had nothing better to do until my audition next week, anyway. And it only cost me plane fare and car rental since Paul is giving me my room for free."

"What about meals?" Pru asked

"A burger doesn't cost much," he said negligently. "And Paul provides breakfast. I can certainly afford to pay for my own food while I'm here."

"That's good," Martha said. "You must have made a lot of money in Hollywood over the years."

"You'd think so, wouldn't you?" He grimaced. "Unfortunately, when you're young and you get the leading part in a TV movie, you really think you've got it made and you spend all the money you make, because you're sure there's going to be plenty more coming in. And then you don't get the

133

next audition – or the next. And suddenly you find yourself waiting tables—" he shuddered "—until you're back in favor amongst the casting directors and then you get job after job for a while."

"What are you going to do when you get older?" Martha asked.

"I've already started putting some money away," he admitted. "On the other hand, other actors my age will have retired or just given up on the whole thing, so I might get lucky and get a good part in a TV show as the wise detective or the head doctor of a hospital – who knows? But I can't count on that happening. That's why I asked Tandy if she could get me a part on her new sitcom – that could have really set me up."

"I'm sorry," Pru said.

"I can't believe she's gone." He sounded genuine. "But if you ladies think I killed her, you're way off base. Why would I? She was going to get me an appointment with Trish and I was still hoping that if her pilot was successful she'd be able to get me some kind of recurring role in the series at least. I'm probably the person who most needed Tandy alive."

***

"Poor Tandy," Martha remarked on the short drive home. "I hope Brock was a true friend to her because right now it doesn't sound like it."

"I overheard them talking that night at the church hall, when Brock was asking her for a part in the sitcom. He reminded her that he'd helped her out a while ago with a role."

"That's right. And she bought him a gold watch later to thank him."

"So why would Brock kill Tandy now?" Pru turned into their driveway.

"That's a good question. And we need to confirm with Flora that Brock was telling the truth about practicing lines for his audition in the motel grounds." Martha clambered out of the SUV.

Pru fetched the walker and helped Teddy out of the rear, and they headed to the front door.

"We also have to follow up on Flora's theory," Martha continued. "What if the killer meant to kill her instead of Tandy? I bet there are a dozen people out there who would love to bash her over the head with that tire iron!"

"Flora isn't as easy to get along with as Tandy, but do you really think Flora was the target? Maybe she just wants to imagine that because it gives her more attention."

"That's an interesting point." Martha nodded. "You're real good at observing people. I don't believe that someone stalking Flora killed Tandy by accident, though. Like I told her at the time, surely a stalker would know exactly who he was killing, even in the dark. He'd know the make and model of the car – heck, even the license plate number – and Tandy had blonde hair, not strawberry-blonde or whatever color Flora's is." She peered at Pru's shoulder-length hair. "I think yours is a much prettier color than Flora's – and it's natural."

"Thanks." She smiled. "Didn't Flora also mention a jealous rival or a past paramour?"

"She did." Martha nodded. "But unless we go to Hollywood, I don't know how we're gonna fact check that."

"We could ask Brock."

"Ruff!"

***

That evening at the church hall, everyone turned up – except for ...

"Where's Teddy?" Lauren glanced around the room.

"He was real tuckered out this afternoon," Martha explained. "We had such a busy day investigating, that he was sacked out on the living room floor while we had a quick dinner and I didn't have the heart to wake him."

"That's understandable," Doris sympathized.

"I'm sure we can manage without him," Flora declared. Tonight she wore black woolen pants that looked very expensive, and a sapphire sweater that looked like it cost even more. Pru wondered if it was cashmere – it was soft, sleek, and made her want to splash out on her credit card and spoil herself, and she was usually careful with her spending.

Brock looked as attractive as usual, wearing gray slacks and a black sweater.

"Let's get started." Flora clapped her hands.

Everyone grabbed a chair from the stack at the rear, apart from Brock and Flora. Pru found herself carrying an extra one and Zoe did the same.

"Did you talk to Doris?" Zoe mouthed when their backs were turned away from their instructors.

"Yes," she mouthed back, nodding for emphasis. Then she gave Zoe a thumbs up. Zoe smiled in relief.

Doris played the waitress again in this episode, and Brock

complimented her on her natural way of acting.

"Thanks," Doris replied. Brock had sat next to her in the circle again tonight but Pru noticed that Doris didn't look quite so starstruck.

Flora refrained from interrupting so much, as if she had something else on her mind, and they were able to finish quickly.

"That was great, everyone," Brock announced at the end of the episode. "It's a shame Teddy wasn't here tonight – I would have loved to see you acting with him, Martha."

"Yeah, I wish he was here too," Martha replied, "but he does need his rest at times."

"How old is he?" Flora asked.

"He's around two years old," Pru replied.

Brock's phone buzzed and he excused himself, walking toward the door and talking quietly into the phone.

"I wonder who's called him," Flora pondered. "As far as I know, he doesn't have a girlfriend at the moment."

"What about you?" Zoe winked.

"Me?" Flora laughed, the sound tinkling down an imaginary piano scale. "Darling, we have been – how shall I say …close … in the past, but now we're just good friends."

"That's a shame," Martha remarked. "I think you two would be well suited."

Pru glanced at her but didn't notice any malice in her friend's expression – or voice. And she thought Martha was right.

"We could be," Flora said, "even though I'm a *teensy* bit older than him. But I vowed long ago not to end up as a boring housewife, slaving away over the housework while my husband goes out to work and has after work drinks, and dinners and … that was a role I played, actually, in a movie, far too long ago to even remember the year! And that was a real eye opener, let me tell you."

"What happened to your husband in the movie?" Lauren asked curiously.

"I stabbed him through the heart with a knife because he was unfaithful."

There was a short silence in the hall, everyone's eyes widening. Brock finished his phone call.

"Sorry, everyone. An actor's life is never his own. That was an old director friend giving me a heads up about a new movie he's casting. He said there's a role that would be perfect for me. It's only small but he said the part is crucial to the story so it shouldn't be cut in the editing process."

"Congratulations." Flora smiled.

But was it genuine?

"I still need to audition for it," he said. "I've learnt never to count my chickens, unfortunately. It's next week, so I'm hoping I'll be out of here by then."

Everyone was silent, even Flora.

"I didn't mean it that way," he said hastily. "Lauren, your husband is the lead detective, isn't he? Can you talk to him for me and tell him how important it is that I'm able to get back to LA next week?"

"I'm sure Mitch is doing everything he can to clear you," Lauren said after a moment. "I'll mention your request to him, but it's totally up to Mitch if he thinks you're okay to return to LA."

"Thank you." He gave a theatrical bow. "That's all I can ask for." He turned to Flora. "Now, where were we, Flor?"

Martha stifled a yawn. "Excuse me. Maybe we should call it a night and pick it up again tomorrow if everyone's agreeable?"

There was a chorus of yeses.

"Really?" Flora sounded disappointed. "I'm raring to keep going, darlings."

"I think Martha's right." Pru spoke.

"Yes," Claire agreed.

"I have a special Sunday customer at the salon tomorrow," Brooke said. "Nine o'clock."

"Oh, that is too bad," Flora sympathized. "That reminds me, I must visit your little salon. It sounds so cute."

"You're welcome any time," Brooke replied politely.

"And I must visit your cat café, too." Flora turned to Lauren and Zoe. "And buy one of your pottery mugs to help you out."

"It's kind of you, but Zoe's latest batch has almost sold out," Lauren replied.

"Then I simply *must* take a look!"

Pru helped Doris and the others take the chairs back to the stack at the rear of the hall. Once again, Flora and Brock didn't offer assistance.

"Are you okay?" she murmured to Doris.

"I'm fine." Doris gave her a small smile. "Don't worry about me." She paused. "I guess I'm glad we had that little talk today. Tonight I looked at Brock with new eyes and I think you were right." She sounded a little sad.

"I'm sorry."

"Don't be." Doris touched Pru's arm. "I'm glad you cared enough to say something."

They finished stacking the chairs and returned to the small group by the door.

Brock's phone buzzed again and he pulled it out of his coat pocket. "I'll take this outside." He opened the stout wooden door and disappeared.

"Hey, Flora." Martha trundled the short distance to her. "Someone told me you and Brock were running lines outside the motel."

"Who told you that?" Flora sounded surprised. "I thought we were being quite discreet. But yes, we were. Brock has an important audition coming up and he asked me to help him."

"What sort of part is he trying out for?" Pru asked.

"A good cop," Flora answered.

Martha nodded to Pru, then turned to Flora. "Do you really think the killer murdered the wrong person? You said maybe they meant to kill you instead the other night!"

"Did I?" Flora tried to wrinkle her brow, however whatever she had done to it cosmetically meant she couldn't achieve that feat. "Oh, yes. I was so shocked when you announced Tandy was dead. Poor, darling Tandy!"

"You said you thought it might be a jealous rival out to get you," Pru reminded her, "and they killed Tandy by mistake."

"And why shouldn't it be?" Flora demanded. "I'm a talented actress and I certainly don't look my age, do I?" She swept a hand down her trim figure. "I know how to take care of my hair and my skin, and I could be a famous make-up artist, with what I've picked up over the years in Hollywood."

Pru had to admit that the actress's make-up was flattering and flawless.

"Who is your jealous rival?" Brooke spoke.

"Well, now, I would have to think," Flora admitted. "It could be any one of a number of fellow thespians who are simply envious of me and my success."

"Like who?" Martha urged.

"Well …" Flora tapped her chin with her forefinger, her manicured nail looking polished as ever, a crystal sparkling for attention. "There's always been a big rivalry between myself and Helen. But I heard she retired and moved to Bali because it's so much cheaper to live there. And then there was another rivalry with Rochelle, but that was way back in London, when I starred as Juliet and she was my understudy. Oh, how I wondered if she was going to murder me backstage one night, she was so *desperate* for my role."

"I guess we can rule those two out then," Martha commented.

"Oh, Martha, you are so naughty!" Flora trilled. "Of course, they could have come out of retirement and be trying out for new roles but not having any success because they haven't looked after their face and body like I have, and nobody wants to cast them because they're too old and haggard!"

There was a slight bitterness in Flora's voice and Pru wondered if she was directing it at herself. Although she looked and acted like a glamorous actress, she hadn't had any noteworthy roles – or any roles of late. Was that the feedback she was getting from her auditions, perhaps couched in kinder language?

"And what about your past paramours?" Martha tried.

"Oh, I've had legions of men wanting to marry me!" Flora brightened. "Really, I've lost count of how many marriage proposals I've received. Of course, I was flattered each and every time but I'm more than just a trophy – I'm Flora Forsey, star of stage and screen! I just simply couldn't settle for something less than that."

"Okay." Martha nodded. "So no past paramours you can think of who would want to murder you."

"Oh, Martha, don't be silly. Of course there'll always be someone who just wants me too much and will do anything to have me."

"Like who?" Doris asked.

"I'll have to make a list," Flora said after a moment.

"That's a good idea." Martha nodded briskly. "And when you do, give it to me or Pru so we can investigate the names."

"Not the police?" Flora queried.

"Them too," Martha replied. "Yeah, Mitch can look into the names on your list as well as me and Pru. And Teddy, of course. And then we'll let you know if we find something."

"You're too kind," Flora replied, with a little less enthusiasm.

"What about a stalker?" Pru posed the question.

"Of course I probably have a stalker," Flora replied quickly. "Any successful actress has one."

"Have you noticed anything out of the ordinary lately?" Martha asked.

Flora put a hand to her brow, as if she were acting out a thinking pose.

"LA is just so big these days, darling. My stalker could be out there watching me every second of the day—" she gave a theatrical shiver, "—and I just wouldn't know it."

"So no stalker then." Martha nodded again.

"Oh, Martha!" Flora's laugh sounded a little forced. "You are one of a kind!"

"Have you noticed anything strange since you arrived in Gold Leaf Valley?" Pru asked.

"Unfortunately not." Flora sounded regretful. "Apart from being so surprised that Tandy took this little coaching job in the first place. But needs must, I suppose." She seemed to recall who she was talking to and quickly backtracked. "Not that I haven't enjoyed my time with you, darlings, and it's lovely that Brock is here, too. With our shared knowledge and acting wisdom, I'm sure you'll carry off your TV show admirably, Martha."

There was a short silence.

"I think Martha's show is going to be great," Zoe declared.

"Definitely." Lauren nodded.

"It might even get on TV one day or on a streaming platform," Claire put in. "Didn't that happen to another show?"

"Yeah, I know the one you mean." Zoe mimed a karate chop.

"Ooh, that's good, Zoe. I'll have to get your character to do something like that," Martha said.

"You mean she isn't already?" Zoe giggled.

They all laughed apart from Flora, who looked a little left out.

Brock came back inside, slipping his phone into his coat pocket.

"Are you ready to go back to the motel, Flor? It's getting late."

"Ready, willing, and able, darling." Flora smiled at him.

"Hey, Brock, can I speak to you for a minute before you leave?"

"Of course, Martha." He looked at her attentively. "What is it? Are you going to give Doris a bigger part? She can certainly pull it off." He smiled in a confidential way to Doris, who looked a little embarrassed.

"That's a good thought, but it's about something else. Pru needs to talk to you, too."

"Now that *is* intriguing." He sketched a bow to everyone else. "Excuse me, ladies."

Pru thought she saw Zoe roll her eyes before she joined Martha and Brock at the rear of the hall.

"We wanna ask you if Flora has any jealous rivals," Martha said in a low tone.

"Flor?" He laughed before quickly stopping. "I haven't heard anything about it and believe me, she'd be on the phone to me immediately if it was true. I adore Flor but she does have a tendency to embellish."

"What about any past lovers who want her at any cost?" Pru said.

"Yeah, in case Tandy's death was mistaken identity," Martha added.

"No." He shook his head. "It's true she's had several marriage proposals in the past, but that was a long time ago. These days, men in her age range unfortunately like them younger than Flora."

"That's a shame," Martha replied. "She *is* a good-looking woman."

"True. And she takes good care of herself. But in Hollywood, the men are looking for younger and younger, and not just in their professional life, but in their personal life, too."

"I think that's terrible," Pru spoke.

"I agree," he replied, but she couldn't tell if he really meant it. "But that's just the way of the world, I'm afraid, especially in Hollywood."

"Not in my world," Martha said stoutly.

Pru smiled in agreement. "What about a stalker?" she asked. "Does Flora have one?"

"No. If she had the slightest hint of being followed, she'd be on the phone to me or Tandy straight away, milking the drama out of the situation. You can be sure of it."

CHAPTER 8

The next morning, Pru yawned, walking into the kitchen.

"Late night?" Martha asked mischievously, slathering butter onto her raisin toast.

"I was on the phone with Jesse after we got home," she admitted. He'd called her when she was about to get ready for bed and they'd stayed talking for a while.

"And?" Martha asked eagerly.

"There hasn't been a break in the case," she replied. "He's looking into Flora and Brock's backgrounds, as well as Tandy's but so far everything is as they said it was."

"Really?" Martha's slice of toast was halfway to her mouth. "I think those two exaggerate at times."

"Jesse mentioned that as well." She gave into temptation and reached for a slice of the cinnamon scented treat, popping it into the toaster. "Flora and Brock have worked a lot in the past, but they were never big-time stars. And it seems that Flora was more successful when she was just starting out in England on the stage than when she got started in movies and TV here."

"That's interesting." Martha crunched into the toast. "Yummy," she mumbled. "What about Tandy?"

"Tandy was the most successful out of all of them but she also had some very slow patches in her career."

"Ruff," Teddy said thoughtfully, sitting next to Martha's kitchen chair.

"What about Brock's request to go home this coming week?" Martha asked.

"Jesse laughed when I mentioned that. He said Mitch is checking them out thoroughly. He's also looking into Paul."

"Paul?" Martha's eyes widened.

"Since Paul was one of the last people to see Tandy alive, of course he's going to be checked out." She paused. "That's what Jesse said, anyway."

"How do you feel about that?" Martha probed.

"I don't like it." She shook her head. "I think Paul is a good guy."

Just then, there was a knock on the front door.

"Maybe it's Jesse," Martha suggested. "Tell him he's welcome to eat with us. He can even have some of my raisin toast."

"Thanks."

Teddy scampered along by her side, barking when they reached the front door. She gave a little gasp when she opened it and saw who stood on the doorstep.

"Paul!"

***

"I need your help," Paul said a minute later, sitting in the kitchen with Martha and Pru. Teddy settled back next to Martha's chair, after he'd snuffled around Paul's sneakers for a few seconds.

"Of course." Martha nodded. "What can we do?"

"Mitch was questioning me just now. He keeps asking me the same questions over and over about my lunch with Tandy." He spread his hands helplessly over the table. "But there's nothing else I can tell him. There were other diners at Gary's that lunch time. It's not as if we were alone. And nothing happened between us – it was just a friendly lunch."

"I remember you saying you were hoping it might lead to more," Martha stated.

"Yes." He looked shamefaced. "I felt embarrassed telling Mitch that, thinking that it might make me a bigger target. But it's not like I said anything like that to Tandy. Like I told you, when her agent called her while we were at Gary's, I realized there wasn't much point in asking her out on a date. She was way out of my league."

"And I told you that you never know," Martha replied. "So what did

Mitch say when you told him about you and Tandy?"

"He had an understanding look on his face, but maybe he was faking it," Paul replied. "He might be considered a local by now, especially since he's married to Lauren, but he's still a police detective and he has to do his job."

"You're right." Martha nodded. "I guess that's the same with Jesse, isn't it, Pru?"

"Yes," she replied after a moment. "But Mitch and Jesse are very fair."

"I've always thought so," Paul agreed, "but when you're getting questioned by Mitch in his official capacity, it feels different."

"I can imagine," Martha said. "It's a shame he didn't want to be in my TV show. That reminds me, I need to write a role for you, Paul, like I promised."

"I just hope I'm free to take part in it one day," he replied gloomily.

"Don't worry. With the senior sleuthing club by your side, you have nothing to fear!"

***

Paul stayed a while longer, telling Martha all the questions Mitch had asked him.

"Huh," Martha had muttered at the end of the list. "Mitch is thorough, that's for sure."

"He thinks I did it." Paul held his head in his hands. "I'm sure of it."

"Then he would have arrested you," Pru spoke.

"Do you think so?" he asked hopefully.

"If he had enough evidence," she replied.

"Maybe he's out there now, gathering all the proof he needs." He sat back in the kitchen chair. "But I didn't do it, so what evidence could there be?"

"That's what we're gonna find out." Martha nodded briskly. "I bet he's asked Flora and Brock lots of questions, too."

"But they don't seem too worried," Pru said. "Not during our acting lessons, anyway."

"I saw Brock pacing up and down outside the office this morning," Paul volunteered. "But then his phone rang and he looked relieved. I saw him pull it out of his coat pocket."

"He said a director friend was offering him a role – or was it a chance to audition for a role?" Martha screwed up her eyes in thought. "One of those."

"He also has an upcoming audition to play a good cop," Pru said.

"That's right. Maybe his phone call was about that instead. That's why he wants to go back to Hollywood this week," Martha remembered. "Paul, let us know if you see Flora and Brock acting suspiciously," she ordered. "That could give us a break in the case."

"Do you think they did it?" he asked eagerly.

"It does seem a bit strange that three strangers came to town around the same time and one of them was murdered. And if you didn't kill Tandy, then who did?"

***

"I don't know why Mitch would think Paul killed Tandy," Martha said later that day. They were relaxing in the living room, Pru with an Agatha Christie novel and Martha with the Sunday newspaper. With Paul's visit, they hadn't made it to church but Martha said she was sure Father Mike would understand.

"There aren't many suspects," she pointed out.

"But Mitch hasn't questioned *us*." Martha pouted. "And I'm the one who hired Tandy to coach us."

"But why would *you* kill Tandy? I'm sure Mitch doesn't think of you as a suspect."

"You're right." Martha nodded after a moment. "I hope not, anyway."

"Maybe he's contacted Trish to find out more about Tandy," she suggested.

"Yeah, I bet he has. Okay, that makes me feel better. But I still want to solve this case. I want to do it for Tandy."

"I understand," she said softly.

***

The next morning, Pru shelved books in the library. She'd just gotten to the Ms in the mystery section, when she saw one of her favorite patrons.

"Hi, Ms. Tobin." She smiled at the tall, slim, brown-haired older woman, who wore a flattering outfit of warm looking tan slacks and a cream sweater.

"Hello, Pru," Ms. Tobin greeted her in a friendly way. "I'm just about to pick up my reserved book." She cast a glance around the large room, deserted apart from Barbara clacking softly away at the reference desk. "I heard about your acting coach being murdered – I am sorry."

"Thanks. How did you find out?"

"It's all you hear about at Lauren and Zoe's café," she confessed. "Everyone is talking about it and speculating who the killer is. And of course we're all hoping for a glimpse of Brock and Flora."

"Really?" She kept her voice low so as not to attract Barbara's attention.

"I've seen both of them in various TV shows and movies over the year. Tandy, too. I loved that sitcom Tandy was in years ago, but I have to admit I did find Brock rather appealing in his younger days." Her cheeks flushed slightly. "Listen to me, talking as if I were a schoolgirl."

"He is good looking," she allowed, "even now."

"I can imagine." Ms. Tobin's voice turned dreamy for a moment. "I guess that's how he worked as much as he did, with those good looks and his acting skills. Tell me, how is he in real life?"

"He can certainly act." She thought back to Brock delivering his lines as a bad guy in Martha's script. "And it was good of him to come down here when Tandy asked him, so we'd have a male to read some of those parts. He and Flora mentioned visiting the café but I don't know if they have yet."

"Oh, that is too bad," Ms. Tobin said. "It would be fun to see them in real life and if the locals knew they were there, they might come to take a peek at them, and then that would be a lot more business for Lauren and Zoe. And Annie, of course."

"Of course." She smiled, thinking of Lauren's silver-gray Norwegian Forest Cat with long, soft fur and a plumy tail. She liked choosing tables for "her" customers and "chatting" to them, and she was great friends with Teddy.

"Pru," Barbara suddenly spoke from the reference desk. "Are you able to find Ms. Tobin everything she needs?"

She looked swiftly at her friend.

"Yes, she is," Ms. Tobin assured Barbara. "Pru is very capable."

"Yes." Barbara nodded and returned her gaze to the computer

screen, but Pru thought she glimpsed a slight smile on her boss's face.

"I'd better let you get back to work." Ms. Tobin indicated the novels on the trolley waiting to be shelved. "I'll pick up my book from the reserves section."

"I hope you enjoy it."

"I'm sure I will." Ms. Tobin smiled. "And my cat Miranda will, too. She loves sitting on my lap and reading the pages with me."

Pru waved goodbye to her and returned to the Ms on the shelf. A short while later, a stylishly dressed woman in her thirties strode into the library. After studying the layout, she walked over to the reference desk.

"Are you Barbara?" Pru heard her ask.

"Yes, I am," her boss replied with a professional smile.

"Oh, good. I need some information on advanced Tunisian knitting techniques from the eighteen-hundreds, and my friend said you can research anything!"

"I do my best," Barbara replied modestly, but Pru thought she was secretly pleased with the praise.

The two ladies discussed the request and Barbara clacked away on the keyboard for a while. When the stylishly dressed woman left, a big smile on her face, she clutched a sheaf of papers that Barbara had printed out for her.

She was just about to take her lunch break when Jesse arrived, heading straight to the returns desk.

"Hi."

"Hi." His lips quirked at the corners. "It seems a while since we've actually seen each other in person."

"I know," she replied softly.

"How about Friday night? I should be free."

"That would be great."

"The bistro?"

"Yes."

The bistro was on the edge of town and had good food and a classy atmosphere.

"Do you think Tandy's case will be solved by then?"

"I hope so." He frowned. "We're still looking into Brock and Flora. When we interviewed Flora, she told us Brock was following her to the church hall the night Tandy died and she didn't stop on the way."

"And did he?" she asked.

"So far we only have their word for it. Brock corroborated her alibi, but there aren't any cameras or even street lights where Tandy was found, and no one else in your group drove that way to the hall."

"Why is Paul a suspect?"

His gaze sharpened. "How did you know we're looking into him?"

"He came and saw us yesterday. He's very worried."

"I know he's regarded as a good guy but we have to look into everyone who had contact with Tandy."

"I think Martha is a bit disappointed Mitch hasn't questioned her yet."

Jesse gave a laugh. "Why would Martha want to kill Tandy? If it wasn't for Tandy's friends Brock and Flora turning up, that would have been the end of Martha's – and yours – acting lessons."

"I know."

"Mitch realizes how important Martha's scripts and possibly turning them into a TV show is to her. Although he – we – don't feel we can take part in her show, we both want it to be a success for her – and for you." His gaze softened as he studied her face.

She was conscious they were in the library, but it still felt like a very private moment.

Barbara cleared her throat from the reference desk. "You can take your lunch break now, Pru."

***

"Goody, you're home." Martha brightened when Pru walked into the living room late that afternoon.

"Ruff!" Teddy stood on his hind legs and twirled around in a circle.

She smiled.

"How was work?" Martha asked.

"It was good. Jesse stopped by and we had lunch together. Flora said she and Brock practically drove together to the hall on the night …we found Tandy, so they have an alibi. He and Mitch are still checking Brock and Flora's backgrounds but they're nearly done – they think. And Jesse said there's definitely not even a hint of Flora having a stalker. They checked with the police department there and she hasn't made a complaint."

"So no mysterious stalker mistook Tandy for Flora." Martha nodded. "I wonder when Brock and Flora can go back home – not that I want them to leave yet since we haven't gotten to the end of my episodes. But they might be champing at the bit tonight at class."

"They might be," she agreed ruefully.

"Well, let's have an early dinner and get ready for class," Martha suggested. "If Mitch clears Brock and Flora by tomorrow morning, tonight might be the last evening we have with them!"

CHAPTER 9

Just as they were about to leave for the church hall, Pru's phone buzzed. It was Lauren, wanting to know if they'd left their house yet, explaining that Annie was feeling a little lonely in the evenings since she was at acting class, and Mitch was working late evenings on the case.

"Father Mike said he can come over here with Mrs. Snuggle, and she and Annie could have a playdate with Teddy."

Pru smiled and glanced down at Teddy, who looked eagerly up at her as if he knew exactly what Lauren was saying on the phone, and then looked at Martha.

"What?" Martha mouthed.

She explained, and Martha grinned. "If that's what Teddy wants to do, why not? We can drop him off at Lauren's place on the way to the church hall."

So that's what they did. Father Mike had just arrived with his white Persian, Mrs. Snuggle. She had been a pedigree show cat whose owner was killed. When Father Mike adopted her, she was a very confused and grumpy cat. But his love and kindness had eventually won her over, and now she was devoted to him. And the whole town knew he was devoted to her as well. After being used to not having friends, Mrs. Snuggle was now good pals with Annie, and Teddy.

"Brrt!" Annie greeted them at the door, her plumy tail waving hello. Mrs. Snuggle followed her.

"Ruff!" Teddy executed a play bow, before scampering down the hall. He'd visited Lauren's cottage before.

The two cats raced after him, and they ran around the living room sofa. Pru wasn't sure who was being chased, but they all seemed to enjoy themselves.

"Thanks, Father Mike." Lauren smiled at him. She was dressed warmly in woolen slacks and a plum sweater. "Mitch should be home later tonight but he knows you're here."

"I hope Teddy behaves himself." Martha chuckled. "I know he's gonna have a good time with Annie and Mrs. Snuggle."

"I'll take good care of them all," Father Mike promised. Middle-aged and balding, he was beloved by the whole town.

"Have fun, Teddy," Pru called as they left.

"Ruff!" He sounded a little distracted, trying to jump up on the sofa. Unfortunately, his short Coton legs were no match for Annie's and Mrs. Snuggle's feline athleticism and they trotted along the sofa in front of him. Then Annie jumped down and affectionately bumped noses with him.

"I'm sure they'll be fine," Father Mike said, waving goodbye to them.

"I'm here!" Zoe zipped out of the house next to Lauren's, her pixie bangs a little messy. "What did I miss?"

"Teddy running around with Annie and Mrs. Snuggle," Martha told her.

"Oh, pooh." Zoe sounded disappointed. "That sounds like fun."

"It was," Lauren assured her with a smile.

Pru and Martha led the way in the SUV to the church hall, Lauren and Zoe close behind in Lauren's white compact car. When they arrived, Brock, Flora, Brooke, and Claire were standing outside, blowing on their hands. The January evening had turned very chilly indeed.

"Sorry," Pru called out as she hopped out of the car.

"Last minute playdate," Lauren apologized, opening her car door.

"I didn't know you had children, Lauren," Flora drawled.

"I don't. Not yet, anyway."

"It's a cat and dog playdate." Zoe giggled.

Flora looked mystified and waited for Pru to unlock the door before she was the first one in.

"It's so cold out there." Flora shivered theatrically in her pale blue pashmina, which was draped over her white cashmere sweater. Elegant black slacks and ankle boots completed the ensemble.

"That's why I wear this." Brock swept a hand down his chest.

Pru had to admit he did look smart and dashing in the long, black woolen coat.

She grabbed a chair from the rear and shrugged off her own green wool coat, draping it over the back.

"Am I late?" Doris dashed inside, her hair falling over her brow.

"We just got here," Pru reassured her.

"Oh, good."

She noticed that Doris didn't greet Brock or Flora, but instead helped Pru bring out more chairs from the stack at the rear.

"Now, where were we?" Flora asked, sitting down on one of the black plastic chairs Pru provided for her.

"Where's Teddy?" Brock peered around the room.

"Playdate," Martha, Pru, Lauren, and Zoe chorused.

Brooke, Claire, and Doris giggled.

"That's a shame," Brock replied. "He could be a real drawcard for your series, Martha."

"That's what Tandy said," Martha replied eagerly. "And I've already spoken to Trish about it. And she said to wait until we see how he does when he acts on the screen for real."

"Wise words." Flora nodded. Then she turned to Lauren. "Darling, how much longer will your husband need in order to clear us from the investigation? I do have that appointment with Trish on Wednesday, and I am loath to reschedule it when dear Tandy secured it for me in the first place."

"He's doing the best he can," Lauren replied evenly. "Hopefully it won't be too much longer."

"Good." Brock nodded. "While it's been delightful being here—" he looked directly at Doris, but Pru thought his good looks weren't having the same effect on her "—I'm afraid we do have to get back to the real world of Hollywood. I have two upcoming auditions now – the role of the good cop I've been rehearsing with Flora, and the new movie role my director friend has put me forward for."

"When is that?" Brooke asked.

"They're both later this week," he replied. "So it's imperative I return home before then."

"That's understandable." Martha nodded. "And I'd like to say on behalf of all of us that we really do appreciate you coaching us like this, especially after what happened to Tandy."

"Oh, Martha, that's so sweet," Flora gushed. "Brock and I have had a delightful time here, apart from what happened to poor Tandy. But I do know she would have wanted us to keep helping you for as long as we could."

"Then we should make the most of your time while we can." Claire turned the page of her script. "Where did we leave off last night?"

Pru followed her lead, and so did everyone else. But she noticed that Brock and Flora were the last to flick their pages to the required spot.

But once everyone started reading their lines, the two actors became professionals, Flora not even interrupting as much as she had last week.

"And, scene!" Brock said with a flourish at the end of the episode. "Martha, I think your scripts are a real find. And," he drew in his breath as if to impart something very important, "if you can find the money to pay me, I would love to be part of your cast when you make this into a TV series."

Flora stared at him in surprise for a moment, then gushed, "Oh, yes, I would simply love that, too! Now, which part should I play? What about the—"

"Hold your horses," Martha ordered. "That's real nice of you, Brock, and you, Flora. But first I've got to crowdfund the money and then you'll have to tell me how much you actors get paid. I could ask Trish what she thinks – yeah, that's a good idea. Now, Brock, you could play one of the two not so hot shots – maybe – or a bad guy, because you were real good at reading that bad guy's lines last week. Flora, I'd have to think real hard about what role I could offer you, to make the best use of your talents."

Pru thought Martha was being very tactful.

"I understand." Flora managed to look disappointed and grateful at the same time. "Please let Trish know if you think I'm right for one of the parts. I'm sure she'll be my new agent once she meets me this week."

"I wonder who is going to take Tandy's place in the pilot." Brooke suddenly spoke.

"I've been wondering about that myself," Brock admitted. He turned to Flora. "What about you, Flor?"

"Me?" Flora sounded genuinely surprised. "Do you really think?"

"You did try out for it," Brock reminded her.

"That's right." Flora nodded. "Of course, it would be wonderful if the casting director called me about it, or asked me to audition again, now that Tandy's … gone, but honestly, darling, I haven't given it much thought. I've been busy concentrating on my upcoming meeting with Trish."

They started chatting about crowdfunding, Zoe wondering when they would actually get started setting it up on the Internet. Then they started returning the chairs to the rear of the hall, Pru stacking hers neatly on top of the others. Doris joined her.

"Are you okay?" she asked her friend in a low voice.

"Yes." Doris managed a smile.

"I noticed you didn't look at Brock much tonight, even though he managed to sit next to you again."

"Oh, Pru, you were right about him all along." Doris blinked hard. "He had lunch at Gary's today – by himself – and I don't know if he expected everyone to recognize him or not – but nobody came up to him to ask for his autograph or take a photo with him – maybe the other diners were too polite. Anyway, he was rude to Cindy, his waitress."

"Oh, I'm sorry." She shook her head. Cindy was a young, blonde waitress who was very nice and very popular with all the customers.

"I couldn't believe it. Cindy is so efficient, but I came out of the kitchen with an extra helping of fries for a table since she was rushed off her feet because we were short-staffed today, and Brock complained to her that his burger was overcooked. But when she apologized to him, he brushed her off and said he couldn't wait around for a new one to be grilled and he would just have to eat it as he had a very busy afternoon. And, he told her not to expect a tip!"

Pru's mouth parted.

"And the worst part was, *I* cooked his burger. And it definitely was *not* overcooked."

"I'm sure it wasn't," she replied, knowing Doris was excellent at her job.

"Brock didn't see me in the dining room, I'm sure," Doris continued. "But that's why I didn't want to have much to do with him tonight."

"I understand," she sympathized. "Maybe he received some bad news or just wants to go home to LA, but I am surprised he acted that way."

"So am I," Doris said sadly. "And Cindy told me later he *didn't* tip her."

"I'm sorry."

"Same time tomorrow, everyone?" Martha suddenly called out. "Brock and Flora, are you able to come again tomorrow night? Or do you think you'll be going back to LA?"

"Since Mitch hasn't said a word to us, I suppose we'll be here." Flora glanced at Brock. "I will, at any rate."

"And I will, too," Brock replied quickly. "I just hope tomorrow is our last day here. Not that I don't find your little town charming," he assured them, "but my audition for the good cop is on Thursday and the try out for the movie role is on Friday. Either part could be a real jump start for my career."

"I understand," Martha told him. "And we appreciate you coming back tomorrow night." She turned to the others. "Don't we?"

"Yes," Pru chorused with everyone else.

"And my meeting with Trish is on Wednesday," Flora said hastily. "I simply can't miss it!"

"Maybe you could do some video conference call thing with Trish if you're still here by then," Martha said. "You can even come to my house and use my desktop computer. I think it has a camera in it."

"It has," Pru confirmed.

"That's simply marvelous of you, Martha, darling." Flora brightened a tad. "All Trish has to do is see me in person and I'm sure she'll be sold on being my new agent. And if I can't meet her in the flesh, then video will be the next best option!"

"You could always do that on your phone," Brock said.

"Of course," Flora replied a tad dismissively, "but I think I'll be shown off to my best advantage in a homier atmosphere than my dreary motel room."

There was a short silence.

"Paul does the best he can," Martha told her evenly.

"Everyone in town loves Paul," Zoe said. "He's been here forever and takes good care of his guests. I think his rooms are quite nice."

"I'm sorry. You must forgive me." Flora pulled out an elegant lace-trimmed handkerchief from her pocket and dabbed the corner of her eye. "I didn't mean to be rude. Sometimes I'm just suddenly overwhelmed when I remember what happened to Tandy."

"Maybe it's best we all go home now," Claire spoke. "And come back fresh tomorrow night."

"Yes." Pru sent her friend a grateful smile.

"We've gotta pick up Teddy from your house," Martha told Lauren.

"I have *got* to come and take a look," Zoe said. She turned to Lauren. "Remember kitty day care?"

"I don't think I'll ever forget it."

Pru wasn't sure if the look on Lauren's face was one of

remembered amusement – or something else.

"What's kitty day care?" Doris asked.

"Something that happened a while ago," Zoe replied. "I thought up a way of making extra money by offering daycare for cats but—"

"It got a little out of control," Lauren finished.

"I'd love to hear more about it," Brock said. "Maybe I could have a stab at writing it into a script one day."

Lauren and Zoe glanced at each other and shook their heads.

"Sorry, but I think it's best kept in Gold Leaf Valley," Lauren said.

"Yeah." Zoe zipped her lips.

They both chuckled.

Everyone filed out of the church hall, Martha beside Pru as she locked the stout wooden door.

"We'll wait for you," Lauren called to them, heading to her car.

"Thanks." Pru smiled.

She waved goodbye to Doris who got into her car, the engine chugging into life. Then she put Martha's walker in the trunk of the SUV and turned on the ignition.

"That was nice of you to let Flora use your computer if she needs to," she said.

"It sounds like she might be a bit down on her luck right now," Martha replied. "As long as she doesn't mess with my settings, I don't mind her using it. Plus, I'm doing her a good turn, and you have to admit, she's been doing us one, continuing to coach us like this when I paid Tandy to instruct us."

"True," she replied. *"And* Flora is also paying for her motel room."

"Now I feel even better about letting her video call Trish at my – our – house!"

***

They pulled up outside Lauren's cottage, which was next door to her Norwegian Forest Cat café. The porch light shone warm and golden.

"I wonder what Teddy's up to right now?" Martha mused. "I can't wait to see him having fun with Annie and Mrs. Snuggle."

But all three creatures were cozied up together on a blanket on the floor.

"Hi, Father Mike," Pru greeted him. He looked a little tired.

"Shh." He put his finger to his lips. "They haven't fallen asleep long." He shook his head. "I don't know where they got the energy from but they've been racing around the house most of the evening. Even Mrs. Snuggle."

"That's wonderful." Lauren spoke.

"Yes, it is." Father Mike smiled down at the fluffy white Persian. "It's taken her a while, but with Annie's help, she knows what it's like to be a friend, and I think she likes it."

"I'm sure she does," Pru murmured.

"Yeah." Zoe nodded fiercely.

"I hate to wake Teddy but we've gotta get home," Martha stage-whispered. "Pru's gotta go to work tomorrow."

"I'll try." Pru bent down to the white, fluffy dog – with Mrs. Snuggle's fur as well as Teddy's, they made a picturesque scene, especially with

Annie's silver-gray tabby fur as a pretty contrast.

She gently stroked Teddy's shoulder and he sleepily blinked open his eyes.

"Sorry, but we have to go home now. Acting lessons are finished for tonight."

"Wuff," he mumbled, stirring to his feet and giving himself a little shake.

His movement woke up the cats and they all touched noses together, saying goodbye to each other.

"Would you look at that," Father Mike marveled. "Even Mrs. Snuggle is taking part!"

"That's what love and kindness does," Martha stated.

"And Annie loves Mrs. Snuggle and is glad to be her friend," Lauren added.

"Teddy, too." Martha nodded. "And you've sure shown Mrs. Snuggle a lot of love and kindness yourself, Father."

Pru settled Teddy into the rear of the car and they set off home. Martha had left her porch light on so they weren't returning in total darkness. It was after nine o'clock and only the occasional streetlamp illuminated their way, as well as Pru's headlights.

Once inside the duplex, Pru locked the front door and turned off the porch light.

"Wuff?" Teddy asked, looking up at her, his brown button eyes still looking sleepy.

"We're going to bed now," she told him gently.

"Come on, little guy," Martha said. "I'm bushed. We got through a lot of the script this evening and I want to be raring to go tomorrow night. It will probably be Brock and Flora's last class with us."

"Wuff."

CHAPTER 10

The next morning at breakfast, Pru's phone buzzed. A text from Jesse.

"What does he say?" Martha asked eagerly. "Is he gonna take you out for lunch today? What about dinner? I can always get Lauren to give me a ride to the church hall if you're gonna be late for class tonight."

"Nothing like that," she replied hastily, studying the screen. "The DNA from the tire iron that they found in the cow manure is too degraded to be of any use. And he said they've checked Brock's claim about his auditions for Thursday and Friday this week and he's telling the truth."

"That's a poop about the tire iron." Martha crunched into her fragrant slice of raisin toast. "What about Flora?"

"They've checked with Trish and she does have a meeting arranged with her."

"I could have checked with Trish," Martha grumbled. "She's my agent. I'm sure she wouldn't have minded if I'd called her and asked about Flora. She knows I'm the president of the senior sleuthing club, after all."

"It sounds as if they're going to clear Brock so he can return to LA," she continued after a moment.

"What about Flora?" Martha asked.

"Jesse doesn't say they're *not* clearing her."

"But we're still no closer to finding out who Tandy's killer is." Martha pouted. "And we've been real busy with our acting lessons, so we haven't had time to do our usual sleuthing around – apart from asking Flora and Brock a ton of questions. Plus, I don't see how Paul could have done it."

"Did you speak to Paul yesterday?"

"Nope, but that's a good idea." Martha pointed a piece of toast at her.

"Ruff!" Teddy agreed from his spot by Martha's kitchen chair.

Martha pulled out her phone from her black walker basket and stabbed the buttons.

"Hey, Paul, have you had any more questioning by Mitch? You haven't? That's good. Uh-huh. Yep. You're right. Pru and I – and Teddy—" she glanced down at him "—are doing everything we can to solve this case." A guilty look flashed across her face as she uttered the words. "Uh-huh. Yep. You betcha. Okay. Bye." She ended the call.

"What did he say?"

"Mitch hasn't asked him any more questions, and to let him know if Mitch asks us about him."

"That's good." Pru finished her breakfast and rose. "I have to go or I'll be late."

"And you don't want to do that," Martha agreed. "Barbara is a real stickler."

"But she's fair."

"Yeah." Martha nodded.

"Ruff! Ruff!" Teddy danced around Pru as she headed to the front door. Then his tone changed to a growly bark. "Ruff! Ruff!"

"What is it?" She opened the front door, aware of Martha trundling up behind her.

"Ruff!" Teddy stared at the bunch of brown, dead flowers lying on the doorstep.

"What the—" She gingerly picked up the decaying bunch of chrysanthemums. Straightening, she looked left and then right, but didn't see anyone scurrying away.

"Careful," Martha warned, peering over Pru's shoulder. "Why would someone leave that on our doorstep?"

"There's a card." She plucked out the square, white card, black handwriting scrawled across it.

"Stop poking around or you'll be dead like these flowers."

CHAPTER 11

Pru wanted to stay home with Martha after the disturbing discovery, but her friend shooed her off to work.

"I'll be fine," Martha assured her. "Besides, I've got Teddy. From the way he acted, I'd say that the person had just left."

"I think so, too."

"I'll call Mitch and let him know," Martha continued. "This means we must be getting closer to the truth about Tandy's death!"

She didn't know whether to be glad or sorry.

"Be careful," she cautioned. "I'm sure Barbara will understand if I stayed home with you today."

"Nope," Martha replied stoutly. "I told you, I'll be fine." She glanced down at Teddy. "Won't I, little guy?"

"Ruff!" *Yes!* He answered confidently.

"See?" Martha beamed.

"Well, all right." She allowed herself to be persuaded. "But make sure you call me if anything happens. And report this bunch of flowers to Mitch before you do anything else."

"I will," Martha promised, her expression suddenly serious. "Don't worry."

But Pru did, all morning. She kept glancing at her phone while scanning books at the returns desk, but no call, missed or otherwise, came through from Martha.

Who could have placed that bunch of dead flowers on their doorstep? Why? Did whoever it was really think that would scare them off the trail of the killer? The person obviously didn't know that Martha – and herself – were made of stronger stuff than that. Although Pru was the reluctant one in their investigations, she did like fitting the pieces of the puzzle together. And a bunch of dead chrysanthemums outside the front door wasn't about to scare her off.

***

"Brooke!" Her eyes lit up when she saw her friend enter the library later that morning. She beckoned her over to the returns desk, aware of Barbara studying the large computer screen at the reference desk.

"Hi." Brooke smiled. Her chestnut locks looked freshly blow-dried, and she wore a green sweater and tailored jeans. "I have some free time this morning so I thought I'd borrow a couple of books."

"That's great. But there was something I wanted to ask you." She lowered her voice. "Do you know if Jeff received an unusual order this morning – or maybe late yesterday?"

"No." Brooke crinkled her brow. "He didn't mention anything when I got home from acting class last night. Or this morning when we had breakfast. Why?"

"Well, the thing is …" She quickly glanced over at her boss, but Barbara seemed engrossed in whatever she was reading on the computer screen

195

"…we – Martha and I – received a bunch of dead flowers on the doorstep this morning."

"No!" Brooke took a step back. "Oh, that's horrible. Jeff would never be involved in such a thing."

"I didn't mean he would," Pru said awkwardly, "just that—"

"I know what you mean," Brooke reassured her. "And if he got a request like that he would definitely tell me. He certainly wouldn't have anything to do with delivering something like that, even if the customer told him it was some kind of joke." She hesitated. "Are you sure they were dead? Maybe they're some kind of strange flower that looks dead but is actually not. Or maybe they're a dried flower bouquet? Sometimes the flowers in that sort of arrangement look brown and dead."

"No, it was a bunch of chrysanthemums. The flowers were brown and decayed."

"Brooke, how are you?" Barbara strode over to them, her smart black patent leather shoes not making a sound on the carpet, and matching her outfit of black skirt and white tailored blouse. "Is Pru helping you with whatever you need?" She turned an inquiring look onto Pru.

"Yes." Brooke nodded quickly. "In fact, she was asking my opinion about flowers, because she knows my husband is a florist."

"That's right." Barbara smiled slightly. "His bouquets look very impressive. I notice them when I walk past his shop." She turned to Pru. "Make sure you shelve those returns—" she surveyed the tall stack beside Pru "—before you go to lunch, please."

"I will," she promised.

"Very good." Barbara nodded to Brooke, then returned to the reference desk.

"I'd better grab some books," Brooke whispered. "And I'll ask Jeff about the dead bouquet, in case he's heard about it from one of his florist friends. I'll text you when I find out."

"Thanks." She watched her friend hurry over to the mystery section and pull out two books at random, before bringing them back to the desk.

Pru checked them out for her, noticing one was an older book by Dorothy L Sayers.

"I hope you enjoy them." She tucked the receipt inside the cover.

"Me too. See you tonight at the church hall."

After her friend left, Pru checked her phone again but still nothing from Martha – or Jesse. Had Martha contacted Mitch by now about the dead flowers?

A couple of hours later, just as she finished eating her ham sandwich in the break room, her phone buzzed. She eagerly looked at the screen. It was a text from Brooke, telling Pru that her husband Jeff was just as mystified as she was about the flowers and that he was sorry they received them.

She'd held something back from her conversation with Brooke – the warning note, telling them to stop "poking around". Maybe that piece of information should only be conveyed to Mitch – and Jesse, of course.

Glancing at her phone again, she was disappointed to find out there were no more texts. She dialed Martha, relieved when she heard her voice on the other end.

"Yes, I told Mitch," were Martha's first words. "And he said he'd come and collect the flowers but he hasn't been here yet. Said there's been a burglary at the shop next to the bank. I'm wondering if the burglars were casing the joint to see if they could tunnel their way into the bank from the shop. Maybe there's a weak spot in the floor and they could dig underneath and into the bank vault!"

"That's an interesting theory," she replied. Martha certainly had an impressive imagination.

"That's what I thought." Pru could hear the grin in her voice. "Anyway, me and Teddy are being real good and staying home today. We have to be here for when Mitch comes and pick up this bunch of flowers. We'll see you this afternoon when you get home."

"Okay." She ended the call, glad that her roomies were all right.

After checking her watch, she got back to the returns desk with one minute to spare. Barbara nodded at her in approval, then left the library to take her own lunch break.

Since she'd finished shelving the stack of returns before lunch, she dug out a box of books that had arrived that morning. This was one of her favorite tasks, and she loved reading the descriptions on the back and making mental notes of which novels she'd borrow herself.

"Darling, there you are." She'd been so engrossed in the blurb of a spy thriller that when she looked up, she was startled to see Flora standing in front of the desk. Dressed in another cashmere sweater and woolen slacks, the actress looked like she was on the verge of returning to Hollywood that very minute.

"Hi, Flora." She smiled and set down the book. "How can I help you?"

"I am simply *devastated*," Flora declared. "Brock is allowed to go back to LA but I am not!" She pouted, her lips enhanced with pale pink lipstick that complemented her strawberry-blonde hair. "Do you think you could ask your boyfriend Jesse to have a word with Mitch about this?"

"I can ask him about it," she replied. "I mightn't get an answer right away, though. Jesse and Mitch are very busy right now."

"I understand." Flora nodded earnestly. "But if you could give me an ETA tonight at class, that would be marvelous."

"I'll let you know if I find out anything."

"Thank you." Flora smiled, showing perfect white teeth.

Just then, Pru's phone buzzed and she gave a little start.

"Anyone important, darling?" Flora glanced at Pru's black device. "You can answer it in front of me. I won't mind."

"Well…" She didn't want to be rude, but what if Martha was in trouble?

Studying the screen, she was relieved to see it was from Jesse, saying he or Mitch would pick up the dead flowers that afternoon.

"Good news, I take it?" Flora asked curiously.

"Yes."

Just then, Barbara entered the library. "Oh, Pru, I am sorry about your doorstep surprise this morning. I was just passing Jeff's flower shop and he mentioned it to me when I remarked on what a beautiful bouquet he had in his window."

"Did you get a gorgeous bunch of roses, Pru?" Flora's eyes sparkled. "Were they from your beau Jesse?"

"I'm afraid not," Barbara answered before Pru could. Then she seemed to realize what she'd just said and looked chagrined. "I'm sorry. This is Pru's private business and I'm not a gossip. Forgive me." She strode to the reference desk and sat down.

"Well, now I *am* intrigued." Flora leaned across the counter, her string of pearls swinging toward Pru. "Do tell. You have no idea how boring it is here. Not that I'm not grateful to be of use to you and Martha and your friends. It's very good for me to go back to the basics. And for Brock, of course. But I'm so used to the hustle and bustle of LA. Not much happens in this sleepy little town, does it?

"I wouldn't say that," Pru replied. Had Flora forgotten that her friend Tandy had been murdered?

"So, who sent you the flowers this morning?" Flora asked, her eyes wide with curiosity. "I do so love receiving flowers from an admirer. Is that it? Do you have a secret admirer, Pru?"

"In fact, it's the opposite." She found herself telling Flora about the grim bunch of flowers she found that morning.

"That is *terrible*!" Flora slowly shook her head. "Oh, you poor things. You and Martha. Did Teddy run after the person who left that awful bouquet on your doorstep?"

"No. There was no one around when I picked it up," she replied, regretful that she'd divulged so much.

"What are you going to do now?" Flora asked. "Are you going to stop investigating?"

"I'm sure that's what the killer would like us to do," she replied, "but they obviously don't know us. Martha takes her role of being president of the senior sleuthing club very seriously." And she realized she took her role as amateur sleuth seriously as well.

"I do hope you'll both be careful," Flora said. "Are you going to tell Jesse about it?"

"He already knows," she replied.

"Oh, good." Flora smiled. "That's a relief. Well, I'll see you tonight at the church hall for our final class. I'm absolutely dying to know how Martha's final episode turns out!"

CHAPTER 12

On the short drive home that afternoon, Pru racked her brains, but couldn't remember seeing that particular handwriting that had been on the square white card accompanying the dead flowers anywhere. The script had been quite elegant. Perhaps whoever had sent them – probably the killer – had used a florist out of town? Maybe an hour away in Sacramento? That might be why Jeff hadn't heard any gossip about it yet from his fellow florists. No doubt Mitch would collect the card for evidence, as well as the dead blooms.

When she arrived home, Teddy ran to greet her.

"Ruff! Ruff!"

"Hello to you, too." She scratched him behind the ears. "What have you been up to today?"

"He got the zoomies this afternoon." Martha trundled up the

hall. "He had a good old time racing to the kitchen and back to the living room. Then he needed a rest."

"I can imagine." Pru smiled down at the fluffy white dog, who led them into the living room.

"That was just after Mitch collected the flowers and the card. I've been racking my brain all day trying to figure out if I recognized the handwriting, but nope." Martha sounded a little discouraged.

"Me too. On the way home."

"I bet Barbara kept you too busy during work hours to think about it. Mitch said he'll put some feelers out, but now he's caught up with this burglary as well as Tandy's death. He's gonna get the handwriting on the card analyzed, as well as fingerprints."

"It will have mine on there," she said guilty.

"Mine too. But maybe he can get something useable somewhere from it."

"I hope so."

"But maybe the person who wrote on the card wore gloves," Martha continued. "With all these crime shows they can learn from, they'd be pretty dumb not to."

She sat on the sofa next to Martha and told her about her day, including Flora coming into the library.

"That's curious, Brock being cleared but not Flora." Martha screwed up her eyes in thought. "Huh. But at least she's coming to class tonight. I wonder if Brock is, or if he's already hightailed it back to Hollywood."

"At least he'll be able to make it back in time for his two auditions this week," Pru replied.

"I hope he gets at least one of them," Martha said. "It was good of him to help out for free with our acting classes."

They discussed what to have for dinner that night before getting ready for class.

"What about some of that beef stew I made?" Martha suggested. "It won't take long to heat it up and then we'll have plenty of time to get ready. I can't wait until everyone reads the end of episode six."

"What happens in it?" Martha hadn't allowed her to read that episode except in class with the others.

"You'll see." Martha tapped the side of her nose and gave a mysterious smile.

Pru heated up the pot of stew and started setting the table when there was a knock at the door.

"I'll go," she volunteered, not sure where Martha and Teddy were.

"Ruff! Ruff!" Teddy suddenly appeared in the kitchen doorway and then raced down the hall to the front door.

"I'm checking something on the computer," Martha called out from her bedroom.

"Okay," she answered, opening the front door, her eyes widening in surprise. "Hi, Flora."

"Darling, you'll never guess what's happened." Flora sashayed inside without waiting for an invitation, carrying a fancy designer purse. "My appointment with Trish has been moved up to *right now*! Well, in about ten minutes. And Martha did say I could use her computer to do a video call with Trish. After all, I do want her to see me in my best light." She patted her tousled locks.

"Martha's using the computer now." She ushered Flora along the hallway. "Let me just check with her."

"Of course, darling. I suppose I could always do a video call on my phone here. Your living room simply must be better than my little motel room."

Teddy had been busy sniffing Flora's black ankle boots, then sat on his haunches and looked up at her.

"Ruff! Ruff!"

"You are too simply gorgeous for words, Teddy." Flora smiled down at him. "Trish is a fool if she doesn't take you on as a client."

"Now that's what I like to hear." Martha emerged from her bedroom. "Apart from the fool part. I like Trish."

"So do I," Flora agreed hastily. "At least, from what I've heard about her. That's why it's so important I make a good first impression on her. I was just telling Pru here that my interview with Trish has been moved up to right now! Something about a double-booked appointment." She tsked. "Well, I suppose it happens. That's why I'm throwing myself on your mercy and asking if I could use your computer to do my video call with her."

"Of course." Martha nodded. "I'm not a real expert on it, but I guess you know what you're doing. I've been reading up on the auditioning process and these days it seems some actors film themselves reading the script instead of going to the actual place where the audition is held." Martha led her into the messy bedroom.

"That's right," Flora replied. "It can be very useful, especially if you're filming on location somewhere but you've got an audition back in LA."

"Could Brock have done that if he wasn't cleared in time for his auditions in Hollywood this week?" Martha continued.

"Yes," Flora replied. "And I would have helped him, of course. But, I'm afraid I have some sad news for both of you. Brock has already gone back to LA. He left this afternoon."

"That was quick," Pru commented.

"So I'm afraid it will only be little old me helping you with the acting tonight," Flora said. "But don't worry, I'm sure we'll come about." She turned to Pru. "Darling, have you had a chance to talk to Jesse yet about clearing me?"

She realized with a start she'd forgotten all about that.

"I'll ask him now." She pulled her phone out of her jacket pocket and started texting.

"Marvelous." She turned to Martha. "Now, where shall I sit?" Teddy circled Flora, sniffing her boots again.

"Right here." Martha patted the comfortable looking computer chair in the corner of the room. "You'd better get started if you don't want to be late for Trish. Now, don't mess up any of my computer settings, like my font size or my screen dimensions, because I've got it just right and it took me a while to get it like that."

"Of course." Flora nodded. "Why don't you show me where the video call button is?"

"This is it." Martha leaned over Flora's shoulder and clicked the mouse. Software sprang to life and there was a whirring sound.

"Marvelous. Now, let me find Trish's details." Flora swiveled around in the chair and delved into her leather purse.

Pru had finished texting Jesse, and turned to look at Flora. She frowned. There was something wrong with Flora's fingernails. She thought back to when she first met her at the church hall, and her dramatic entrance. She'd admired the actress's fingernails, pale pink with a tiny crystal in each nail.

Now Flora's middle finger on her right hand did not boast a sparkly crystal, and the side of it looked like it had broken off slightly and been smoothed back into shape. It was no longer a perfect oval like her others, although it looked pretty close.

Her mind flashed back to the night they discovered Tandy. Flora had called Tandy on her cellphone, but only used her thumbs and forefingers on the device. Was that why? To cover up her broken fingernail?

"Flora," Pru said slowly, "what happened to your fingernail?"

"Hmm?" Flora looked up from the depths of her purse. "What fingernail?"

"That one." She pointed to Flora's middle finger. "Did you snag it somewhere?"

Flora squinted at the pink nail. "Oh, yes, I'm afraid I did it on the plane, trying to stow my bag into the overhead locker."

"Huh." Martha frowned. "That's not how I remember your fingernails. I thought to myself on the night you arrived at the church hall, surprising us all, how good your nails looked. Not like mine." She looked ruefully down at her short, stubby nails.

"Yes." Pru nodded emphatically, then turned to Martha. "That's exactly what I was thinking that night."

"Ruff! Ruff!" Teddy circled the computer chair, staring up at Flora in a challenging way.

"Maybe it happened later and I didn't notice." Flora shrugged and reached inside her purse again.

"I don't think so," Martha said. "I may be in my seventies, but my memory's not that bad."

"Neither is mine," Pru agreed.

"Unfortunately for both of you." Flora pulled a gun out of her purse and aimed it at them. "Why did you have to stick your nose into my business? Everyone I met in this dinky little town told me about your senior sleuthing club and how you're determined to solve every mystery that happens here!"

"Ruff!" Teddy growled, showing his teeth.

"And you can keep that mutt away from me, or he'll be the first to go." Flora bared her own gleaming white teeth at him.

"It's you!" Martha pointed a finger at Flora. "You killed Tandy! But why?"

"She deserved it," Flora snarled. "Everyone thinks Tandy was some kind of saint, such a lady, so well-spoken, blah, blah, blah. Well, let me tell you something. Years ago, when we were both starting out, although I'd had more experience than her back then – this is after I came to Hollywood from England, lured by that movie role. Well, after that, my career slowed down. I still don't know why. And suddenly I found myself struggling to get work. I met Tandy at a coffee shop and we hit it off – until she did something *terrible*."

"What?" Pru asked. She and Martha – and Teddy – stood in front of Flora, who faced away from the desk, still sitting in the computer chair. There was no way she could take Flora by surprise – at least not yet.

"We were both auditioning for the same movie role – and this role was my chance to be on top again. Or near the top, anyway. And this would have been Tandy's big break – in fact, it was. We both had the same agent back then as well – and Tandy told me she'd just gotten a call from our agent telling her the venue had been changed and to let me know, as our agent knew we were friends. I'd been late paying my phone bill that month and they'd cut me off, so I couldn't use my phone to check with our agent that it was true. Besides, I trusted Tandy – until then she'd been kind to me and had even lent me a few dollars when I needed it."

"But wouldn't you be rich from your movie role?" Martha interrupted.

"Ruff!"

"That role didn't pay as much as it should have," Flora replied bitterly. "And because everyone was telling me I was going to be a big star, I blew through the money faster than I imagined." She shook her head. "I still have a craving for pretty things." She waved a hand down her expensive cashmere attire. "I wish I could be happy living in sweatsuits like you, Martha." She glanced at Martha's turquoise sweatpants and matching sweater. "Or ordinary clothes like you, Pru." She gave a dismissive look at Pru's outfit of gray slacks and white shirt.

"What happened?" Pru urged, caught up in the tale, despite the danger they faced.

"Tandy told me a big fat lie! I went to the new venue for the audition and it was empty! It was a church hall on a deserted street, but there was no one there. I couldn't call my agent since there were no payphones, so I couldn't find out if the location had changed at the last minute. When I saw Tandy that evening I asked her about it and she said they'd changed the venue again at the last minute and she had no way of contacting me in time. And Tandy got the part!"

"Weren't you happy for her?" Martha asked.

"I suppose so," Flora replied grudgingly. "I'd rather her get it than someone I hated, but I always had my suspicions about what had really happened that day. That Tandy had lied to me because I was her biggest competition."

"Really?" Pru's eyes widened. Then she remembered Tandy telling them that she had done some things in her past that she hadn't been proud of. Was this one of them?

"That movie role was her big break," Flora continued. "Meanwhile, I kept struggling until I got some work, and for a while things were okay career wise for me. Even Tandy went through some slow patches in her career. But if I'd gotten that role instead of her, just imagine where I'd be now! I'd probably have won at least one Academy Award, if not two!"

"Is that why you killed her?" Pru asked.

"That's not the only reason," Flora replied. "Tandy always made a big deal about being *au naturel* and not having any work done to her face. Actresses younger than her have had plastic surgery, whether they admit to it or not. Even I've had a few little tweaks here and there."

"You can't tell," Martha said admiringly.

"Thank you." Flora smiled smugly. "That's because I go to the best, even though it costs an absolute fortune. And most people don't know who the best is, even though they think they do."

"But Tandy did have a major cosmetic procedure, didn't she?" Pru asked.

"Yes." Flora's eyes flared. "After saying she would never go through such a barbaric experience. She knew we were up for the same role in the new sitcom, playing the glam granny. I thought I was pretty much a shoo-in – my body of work speaks for itself. And I still have my looks." She patted her artfully tousled strawberry-blonde hair with her free hand. The other still pointed the gun at them, strong and steady.

"But then Tandy goes and gets a facelift so she looks even younger than me, even though I'm younger than her! *AND SHE GETS THE PART!*"

219

"I can see how that upset you," Martha said.

"You bet it did!" A rougher British accent emerged from Flora's mouth.

"But why did you come all the way to Gold Leaf Valley then?" Pru couldn't help asking.

"To confront her. And that happened on the way to the church hall that fateful night. It was the first time I was able to be alone with her – she avoided me when we were at the motel. At first I thought I'd done something to upset her – ha! And then I realized she must be feeling guilty about what she did to me. Once again, she cheated me out of a big role!"

"By getting a facelift?" Martha quizzed.

"And lying about it beforehand! Nobody knew she was getting one until she arrived at the audition – or so I was told. And they loved her – and her new face! So of course she got the part and poor little me was out in the cold – once again! So when I saw her car on the side of the road –

she had a flat tire – I saw my chance. I stopped and pretended I was going to help her and I grabbed the tire iron. But before I whacked her over the head with it, I made her admit what she'd done to me all those years ago, by lying to me about the venue change for the audition."

"And she confessed?" Pru asked.

"Yes," Flora replied, grim satisfaction in her voice. "And that's all I needed to kill her. I must have snagged my fingernail on the tire iron and the crystal fell off. I spotted it on the ground and picked it up. Then I did a quick repair job on my nail while I drove to the church hall – I always carry my make-up bag with me."

"Did you leave the dead flowers on my doorstep?" Martha demanded.

"Yes!" Flora smirked. "I got worried last night when I was asked if I was going to get the glam granny part in the pilot now that Tandy was dead. I bumped into Paul from the motel when I got home last night and he said you and Pru were going to clear his name. So early this morning I went to the cemetery and grabbed a bunch of dead flowers." She tsked. "Someone really should take better care of the offerings people leave there.

"That's why I visited the library today, to winkle out from Pru what your reactions had been. If the bouquet had stopped you from your "sleuthing" then I wouldn't be here right now."

"You mean you don't have a video call with Trish tonight?" Martha asked.

"No, darling," Flora drawled. "That was a ruse to come inside. And you fell for it!" She levelled the gun once again at them.

"Gruff! Gruff!" Teddy growled fiercely

"But what about your alibi?" Pru asked desperately. "Didn't Brock say he followed you on the way to the church hall that night?"

"I asked him to lie for me," Flora replied simply. "And of course, he did, because he realized he didn't have an alibi, either. And since he thought there was no way I would kill Tandy, even though he was aware of our – how shall I put it – rivalry – he was happy to go along with it. He told me he put on a masterful performance during his police interview. Hmm. Maybe that's why he got cleared ahead of me."

"I can see how Tandy moving ahead with her career would make you real angry." Martha nodded. "You could write a big-time movie about all this."

"Maybe I will one day," Flora replied. "With all the details changed, of course, so nothing can be traced back to me. But first, I have to kill you." She aimed the gun a little higher at them, pointing at their chests.

"Pru will go first, in case she thinks she can outsmart me in some way. Then you, Martha. I'm sorry I have to kill you, because I think your TV show scripts are quite good. You might even have a chance to really do something with them. And I would love to be in them. But now Tandy's

223

gone, I could be getting a second chance at playing the glam granny in the pilot." She frowned, her forehead not moving. "It's a wonder my agent Hal hasn't called me about it. The producers must know by now that Tandy's dead."

"What about Teddy?" Pru cleared her throat.

"Of course he will have to go, too." Flora glared at the white fluffy dog, who stared up at her angrily, his hackles raised. "I believe it's true when they say dogs remember things. And he'll remember that I killed both of you. He might not be able to speak, but he's a clever thing. And I certainly don't want him to bite me." She shuddered.

"Why don't you put down the gun?" Martha said hoarsely. "Maybe we can do a deal. You can even be the retired lady detective in my show if you don't hurt us."

"Do you mean it?" Flora lowered the gun slightly, hope in her voice. Then her eyes narrowed. "I've played enough TV movie roles to realize this is a trick." She aimed the gun higher, at their heads.

"You're right," Martha admitted. "I don't do deals with killers. But you have to admit it was a good try."

"What about our bodies?" Pru tried to buy some time. Her heart hammered and her stomach twisted. "What are you going to do with them?"

"I'll leave them here for someone else to discover." Flora laughed harshly. It was not a pleasant sound. "You certainly have a lot of crime happening in this town, with the store being burgled and people being murdered. The police will probably think it's a home invasion."

"We don't have home invasions in Gold Leaf Valley!" Martha sounded outraged.

"But you do seem to have a lot of burglaries from what I've heard," Flora replied. "Maybe the burglars are branching out."

"Ruff!" Teddy made a sudden lunge at Flora's ankle boots.

"Call your dog off." Flora pointed the gun at his head. "Or else."

"Teddy, come," Martha said hoarsely.

With one last glare at Flora's ankles, Teddy reluctantly returned to Martha's side.

"Good boy." Martha bent down stiffly to pat him.

"Very touching," Flora sneered. "But now your time has come. Hmm. Maybe I should include that one day if I write a script myself." She pointed the gun at Martha and Pru. "Okay, Pru, I want you to kneel down with your hands in the air. No funny business. It will look more like a home invasion this way."

"How is she going to do that if she can't use her hands to help her onto the floor?" Martha frowned. "I hope you're not gonna ask me to do that. There's no way I can get down on the carpet without help."

"It's true," Pru agreed, telegraphing a desperate look at Martha. If Flora forced her to kneel, then she might be able to catch her off balance by sweeping her leg out in a surprise move.

"Don't you teach yoga?" Flora demanded. "You should be limber enough to do something so simple. Kneel down – now!"

With a sidelong glance at Martha, Pru slowly bent her knees. Thank goodness for her yoga practice. When she was almost to the floor, she suddenly swept out her leg, catching Flora's foot.

"Ow!" Flora jerked, her gun hand casting a wide arc and the revolver pointing at the floor. Before Pru could jump up, Martha grabbed her phone from her walker basket and threw it hard at Flora's head.

"Ow!" Flora put up her free hand to her temple. "That hurt!"

"Ruff! Ruff!" Teddy lunged at her, attacking her ankles clad in the leather boots, while Pru snatched the gun dangling from Flora's hand.

"Now it's your turn to put your hands up," she told Flora with grim satisfaction.

"Yeah!" Martha pointed an imaginary revolver at Flora.

EPILOGUE

The next afternoon, Pru still felt a little shaken whenever she thought of the events that had occurred in Martha's bedroom.

After they subdued Flora, Pru had called Jesse, who raced to the scene, along with Mitch. She and Martha watched Mitch handcuff Flora and march her out of the house.

Jesse took their brief statements and said he'd be back later that evening, before promising to update them the following day.

And now he was here, in Martha's living room, a cup of hot chocolate in his large, capable hands, sitting on the cheery yellow sofa between Martha and Pru. Teddy sat at Martha's feet, resting his head against her legs.

"The reason we hadn't cleared Flora yet," he explained, "was because we weren't satisfied with her explanation about her fingernail, although she sounded plausible. She said she damaged one slightly when she was walking in the park one day, and stumbled over a rock and put her hands out to save herself, and what she'd held onto was a tree trunk. And since Brock backed up her alibi and he was very believable, we didn't have enough to arrest her. But we knew she was Tandy's rival, and had a good motive to kill her. She's almost out of money, and getting Tandy's TV pilot role would have been a big boost for her."

"Where did Flora get the gun from?" Pru asked.

"She told us that she disguised herself as an *ordinary person* – her words – and asked around the seedy edges of town and managed to find someone willing to help her. We're going after him, too."

"What's going to happen to Brock?" Martha asked.

"He was interviewed last night in LA. Once he discovered that Flora had confessed to you that she killed Tandy, he said the fake alibi had been Flora's idea, and he'd only gone along with it so he wouldn't be under suspicion. The LA detectives said he seemed genuinely upset that Flora had killed Tandy. He'll probably be charged with giving false information to us, but in the meantime he'll be able to make those auditions this week."

"He'll be pleased about that." Martha nodded.

"No doubt Thelma from *The Gold Leaf Valley Gazette* will want to ask you some questions." Jesse took a sip of his hot chocolate. "Her article about Tandy will be in Friday's edition."

"Poor Tandy," Pru murmured.

"Yeah, she was a real lady," Martha added. "Okay, she did something bad when she was younger by playing that audition trick on Flora, but she definitely felt guilty about it. She told me." She turned to Jesse. "Just before she died. Said she always regretted something she did in her past."

Jesse nodded.

"What's going to happen now with your retired lady detective scripts?" Pru took a sip of her own hot cocoa. "And what happens at the end of episode six?"

"I still wanna make my show, with all of you in it. And at the end of episode six, my retired lady detective finds one of those two not so hot shots dead – or is he?" Martha gave Pru and Jesse a mischievous look.

"Ruff!"

THE END

If you sign up to my newsletter, you'll receive a Free and Exclusive short story titled **When Martha Met Her Match.** It's about Martha adopting Teddy from the animal shelter, and it's the first title in Martha's Senior Sleuthing Club series!

Sign up to my newsletter here: **www.JintyJames.com**

If you already receive my newsletter and didn't receive the short story, please email me at **jinty@jintyjames.com** and mention the email address you used to sign up with, and I'll send you the link.

Please turn the page for a list of all my books.

TITLES BY JINTY JAMES

Senior Sleuthing Club Series:

Book Clubs Can Be Fatal – A Senior Sleuthing Club Cozy Mystery – Book 1

Garage Sales Can Be Fatal – A Senior Sleuthing Club Cozy Mystery – Book 2

Yoga Can Be Fatal – A Senior Sleuthing Club Cozy Mystery – Book 3

Fortune Telling Can Be Fatal – A Senior Sleuthing Club Cozy Mystery – Book 4

Game Shows Can Be Fatal – A Senior Sleuthing Club Cozy Mystery – Book 5

Jelly Donuts Can Be Fatal – A Senior Sleuthing Club Cozy Mystery – Book 6

Sneaky Snooping Can Be Fatal – A Senior Sleuthing Club Cozy Mystery – Book 7

Mistletoe Mischief Can Be Fatal – A Senior Sleuthing Club Cozy Mystery – Book 8

Norwegian Forest Cat Café Series:

Purrs and Peril – A Norwegian Forest Cat Café Cozy Mystery – Book 1

Meow Means Murder - A Norwegian Forest Cat Café Cozy Mystery – Book 2

Whiskers and Warrants - A Norwegian Forest Cat Café Cozy Mystery – Book 3

Two Tailed Trouble – A Norwegian Forest Cat Cafe Cozy Mystery – Book 4

Paws and Punishment – A Norwegian Forest Cat Café Cozy Mystery – Book 5

Kitty Cats and Crime – A Norwegian Forest Cat Café Cozy Mystery – Book 6

Catnaps and Clues - A Norwegian Forest Cat Café Cozy Mystery – Book 7

Pedigrees and Poison – A Norwegian Forest Cat Café Cozy Mystery – Book 8

Christmas Claws – A Norwegian Forest Cat Café Cozy Mystery – Book 9

Fur and Felons - A Norwegian Forest Cat Café Cozy Mystery – Book 10

Catmint and Crooks – A Norwegian Forest Cat Café Cozy Mystery – Book 11

Four-Footed Fortune – A
Norwegian Forest Cat Café Cozy
Mystery – Book 19

Rewards and Revenge – A
Norwegian Forest Cat Café Cozy
Mystery – Book 20

Catnip and Capture – A Norwegian
Forest Cat Café Cozy Mystery – Book
21

Mice and Malice – A Norwegian
Forest Cat Café Cozy Mystery – Book
22

Prowling at the Premiere – A
Norwegian Forest Cat Café Cozy
Mystery – Book 23

Maddie Goodwell Series (fun witch cozies)

Spells and Spiced Latte - A Coffee
Witch Cozy Mystery - Maddie
Goodwell 1

Visions and Vanilla Cappuccino - A Coffee Witch Cozy Mystery - Maddie Goodwell 2

Magic and Mocha – A Coffee Witch Cozy Mystery – Maddie Goodwell 3

Enchantments and Espresso – A Coffee Witch Cozy Mystery – Maddie Goodwell 4

Familiars and French Roast - A Coffee Witch Cozy Mystery – Maddie Goodwell 5

Incantations and Iced Coffee – A Coffee Witch Cozy Mystery – Maddie Goodwell 6

Made in United States
North Haven, CT
09 January 2025

64199164R00145